Limpy

Limpy

The Boy who felt Neglected

By

William Johnston

Ross & Perry, Inc.
Washington, D.C.

Ross & Perry, Inc. Publishers
216 G St., N.E.
Washington, D.C. 20002
Telephone (202) 675-8300
Facsimile (202) 675-8400
info@RossPerry.com

SAN 253-8555

Library of Congress Control Number: 2002106278
http://www.rossperry.com

ISBN 1-932080-47-3

Book Cover designed by Sapna. sapna@rossperry.com

" I'll be Captain Kidd," continued Jim, " and you be Peg-leg, the sailor." FRONTISPIECE. *See Page 181.*

CONTENTS

LIST OF ILLUSTRATIONS

"LIMPY"

CHAPTER ONE

A WONDERFUL DISCOVERY

THE battle of Gettysburg was about to be fought over again in Tucker's back-lot. Bob Tucker, as became the son of the man who owned the biggest mansion in the neighborhood, was running things, with Froggie Sweeney, his Pythias from a humbler home, assisting.

"I'll be General Pickett," Bob announced.

"An' I'll be General Lee," said Froggie.

"Now, you can't be General Lee. Both him and Pickett was rebels. We can't have a battle with all rebels."

"T'ain't right to call 'em rebels," objected Henry Randolph Peters. "They wuz Confederates. My mother's uncle from Virginia's visitin' at our house, and he fought in the war.

He always calls 'em Confederates, an' I guess he knows."

"Confederates and rebels is all the same thing," decided Bob. "Maybe they wuz Confederates in Virginia, but as soon as they come North they wuz rebels. Who are you goin' to be, Froggie?"

"I'd ruther be Lee nor anybody else, General Robert E. Lee."

"We've got it on our phonograph. It's a bully record," wheezed Fatty Bullen, who had just arrived.

"Aw, shut up! We ain't givin' a concert. We're planning a war," Bob Tucker explained reprovingly. "We're playin' Gettysburg."

"What's a steamboat got to do with Gettysburg?" demanded the rebuked Fatty, thick in brain as in body.

"Aw, shut up!" growled Tucker once more. "Come on, Froggie, who are you goin' to be?"

Froggie pondered. American history, as well as geography, spelling, grammar, arithmetic, and good conduct, were weak points with him. "I don't know no more generals," he complained.

A peaked, slender youngster, one leg clamped tight in a cruel iron brace, who had been hovering excitedly on the edge of the group, worked his way in a little nearer the leader, eyes shining and lips trembling with knowledge unspoken. Froggie Sweeney might be found wanting in information about the famous battles of American history, but not so Edward Haverford Randall. In his puny body dwelt a martial soul. He knew the names of all the commanders, North and South, and could have told most of the battles they had won and lost. Debarred by his deformity from sports in which the other boys delighted, and easily tired out whenever he endeavored to compete with them, he spent far more time in reading than do most youngsters of his age, and to pass away the monotony of his enforced and frequent solitudes had invented for himself many varieties of mental amusements. Often and often he had played that he was General Pickett making his famous charge.

"And if I only had a horse," he would comfort himself, "I could ride and gallop as well as any one, and nobody would know about It."

Poor sensitive little soul, even in his confidences with himself he never referred to his crippled leg in any other way than just It —

a terrible, terrible It, the shaming consciousness of which seldom left him for a single one of his waking moments. But now, in the excitement of approaching battle, self was for the time forgotten. He limped eagerly up to Froggie Sweeney.

"General Meade was a Union general," he burst forth. "He com——"

"Good for you, Limpy!" Bob Tucker interrupted. "All right, Froggie, you be General Meade."

The absorbing business of enlisting the rival armies forthwith began. Eddie, in his anxiety to participate, forgot for once to be mortified at his unwelcome nickname.

"I'll take Dick," said Bob.

"An' I'll take Cookie," said Froggie.

"I'll take Fatty."

"I'll take Four-eyed."

"I'll take Pete."

"I'll take Tom."

As one after another of the boys was chosen, and he still left, the very panic of despair that seized the little lame boy gave him unusual boldness. He could not believe it possible that they were going to leave him out of it. It was he who had told them about General Meade.

It was his game they were about to play.   He *must* be in one or the other of the armies.

"You'll pick me, won't you, Bob?" he asked with sudden resolution, as General Bob Tucker Pickett's choice wavered between the two other boys left beside himself.   They were "littler fellows," hardly worth picking.

For answer Bob eyed him with a surprised stare.   "Naw, of course I ain't going to pick you!   You can't run fast enough to play battle.   You're too lame," he added with the brutal candor of youth.

In spite of his mightiest efforts the tears welled up in the eyes of Edward Haverford Randall.   He did so want to play Gettysburg! Even Bob Tucker, boy-brute that he was, relented as he saw the passionate longing expressed in the little cripple's drawn face.

"Tell you what, Limpy," he said not unkindly, "you can play the killed and wounded. More'n three-fourths of Pickett's men was *casualties*.   You be the killed and wounded. It'll just suit you."

"I won't," Eddie managed to blurt out with firmness, as he turned and strutted crookedly away, his head held high that the fellows might not suspect the presence of the great tears that were rolling down his cheeks. Play "killed and wounded"— he who had so often pretended that he was the great General Pickett, he who knew the story of the battle by heart! "Killed and wounded!" Not much. There would be no fun for him in playing that.

Tucker's back-lot joined Eddie's home, and thither the boy, seared to the heart by the unwitting cruelty of his mates, blinded by his own bitter tears, made his way. Twice he stumbled and fell, each time the cruel iron rods that bound his leg giving it a painful wrench, which, in the intensity of his mental anguish, he hardly heeded. Unerringly some subconscious instinct sent him now in search of woman's sympathy, for, since the world began, in time of trouble as in time of joy the man ever has sought the woman; the husband, the wife — the young man, the maid — and the boy, his Mother.

Generally at this time in the afternoon Mrs. Randall was to be found alone in the little sewing-den that overlooked the side-porch, her darning-basket in her lap, busy with the never-ending succession of holes in the hosiery of the four of them—Dad, his two older brothers, and himself—but never too busy to put aside her

work-basket and gather into her arms which-
ever of her four men, as she called them, sought
solace.

Even as he clambered awkwardly and painfully up on the porch a fresh pang of grief shot
through his heart. He heard the shouts with
which General Bob Tucker Pickett, his forces
galloping at his heels, charged across the wheat
field—the Tucker strawberry bed, to be exact
— and he heard the answering yells with which
General Froggie Sweeney Meade and his
Union troops rallied to repel the invaders.
Great silent sobs shook the boy's puny frame.
The intensity of his grief brought all manner
of morbid thoughts into his head. No one
wanted a little lame boy in any of the games.
He wished he was dead. He never, never,
never, could be like other boys, and run and
jump. What if he did know all about General Meade and Gettysburg? Bob and Froggie would neither of them pick him on their
side. In all their games he was always the last
one chosen, if indeed he was chosen at all. Nobody ever wanted him. Nobody cared anything about him, that is nobody besides Mother.
She always wanted him, always welcomed him.

As he crept along the porch, his poor lame

leg dragging pitifully, through the open window of the sewing-room a strange voice came
drifting out; he stopped abruptly. It was
" callers." He never liked them. They
looked pityingly at him. If they knew about
" it " they asked him how his leg was. If they
didn't know — it was worse. " How did you
hurt your leg, little boy? " they were sure to
say. He never appeared when there were
visitors if he could avoid it.

" Is Eddie's leg any better? " he heard a
woman's voice asking.

" He's still very lame," he heard his mother
answer. " We are doing everything we can
for it, but he has to wear a brace. I'm afraid
he will have to wear it always."

Oh, how could she! It did not seem possible that it could be his own dear mother thus
calmly discussing him with a stranger. Surely
she must know how it shamed and mortified
him to have " it " talked about by any one.
He hated any mention of " it " when only his
dad and the boys were present. Surely, surely
she would not talk any more about it. All unconscious of the little listening wraith of grief
outside the screens Mrs. Randall continued:

" Of course Eddie can not play very much

with the other boys. It tires him too much; but he doesn't seem to mind. He sits and reads most of the time."

"Doesn't — seem — to — mind!" His mother's words cut deep into the shame of his loneliness. Even she did not realize the anguish that his crippled limb brought to him. An unwonted sense of bitterness toward her swept over him. Even she didn't care! How could she, when she kept on talking about "it" to a strange woman. His tears dried up in anguish too great for expression. Sick at heart, feeling wretched and miserable and unwanted, he hobbled as silently as he could away from the window and down off the porch.

He stood pondering over his troubles, the craving for human sympathy strong upon him, yet with the feeling that with the refuge of his mother's arms denied him there was no place else in all the world for him to go. From the direction of the tool-house in the barn came the voices of Dad and his two brothers, Tom and Richard.

Boyhood's griefs are evanescent. He wondered what they could be doing there. The continuing sound of their voices stirring his curiosity further, he lent himself to his new impulse and limped slowly across the lawn to peer in at the open tool-house.

Dad was at the work-bench hammering down a rivet in the strap of a leather knapsack. The two boys were watching him and excitedly discussing a " hike," on which the three of them were going to start early the next morning. In the joy of a new enthusiasm Eddie forgot his troubles.

" Oh, Dad!" he cried with kindling eyes, " can I go too?"

" Nothing doing, son," replied Mr. Randall, busy with the refractory rivet. " We're going to Bear Pond, and it's too far for you to walk. It's a good five miles each way, and you're too lame to make it."

Absorbed in his task, the father did not see his little son's eager look give way to one of uttermost despair. Little did he suspect with what harshness his carelessly uttered refusal had struck into the depths of the little crippled boy's over-sensitive soul. Yet the blasting of Eddie's new hope had brought back to him more vividly than before all his other troubles, making of them a burden that seemed wholly unbearable.

Nobody wanted him — nobody! The boys

had refused to let him play Gettysburg with them. His mother had sat there calmly discussing him with some strange woman. She could not have done that if she really and truly loved him. Even Dad — his wonderful, strong, youthful-looking Dad — spurned his company. A new resolve filled him. He would show them all. " Couldn't walk that far," couldn't he? He would show them! He would run away. He would walk and walk, until they never could find him. Maybe then they would be sorry.

His one thought was for an immediate start without detection. As he hobbled away from the tool-house he tried to assume an air of don't-care-ness, and even bravely puckered his lips in an effort to whistle, but somehow the whistle would not come. To escape observation he made for an unofficial opening at the corner of the lot. As he squeezed through to the sidewalk he noted with satisfaction that *She* was out on the porch of the house next door.

The family there had moved in only two days before. Yesterday he had seen her for the first time, a dainty, fairylike creature, all ribbons and frills, with golden curls that reached to her waist. All the previous afternoon he had worshipped afar off, saying to himself that she was the prettiest girl ever he had seen, wondering what her name was, speculating on how he was to get acquainted. She might have been a fairy princess — had he believed in fairies.

Now at the sight of her he squared his shoulders and endeavored manfully to hide his limp, succeeding only in attaining a pathetic, lopsided strut. His heart beat fast with excitement when he saw that she was regarding him with interest. He slackened his pace a little as he observed that she had arisen from the porch where she had been playing with her dolls, and was coming toward him. He could not believe it possible that this vision of loveliness really was going to condescend to speak to him.

" Hello, little boy," she called out, in a voice such as a queen would have.

He stopped abruptly, too confused and overwhelmed to know just what he was doing. She stood regarding him intently, as the color mounted to his cheeks, and his heart kept beating faster and faster.

" What made you lame? " she demanded

"What made you lame?" she demanded suddenly. *Page 12.*

suddenly with the vicious directness of eight.

"I'm not lame," he shouted angrily, as he fled crookedly up the street, his resolve to run away fortified by this new mortification.

He decided now that he would walk and walk and walk until he had walked himself to death. When he couldn't go any farther he would just lie down and die. Maybe then they would all be sorry. As his weak, weary legs dragged him on and on his cheeks still tingled at the shame of the fairy princess's insult, and his mind was filled with morbid, ghastly thoughts. He tried to picture to himself how Dad would look as he was carried back into the house dead. Mother, he knew, would cry. She had cried for two whole days when Aunt Mary died. Perhaps the little girl from next door would come in to look at him, and, oh, wouldn't she be sorry then!

Absorbed in his melancholy imaginings, he had kept on traveling until he was much further away from home than he ever had been before in this direction. As he followed the street down through the culvert that led under the railroad tracks he noted, not without a feeling of timidity, that he was in wholly unknown territory. The houses were much smaller and more dingy-looking than those nearer his home. Here and there was a little shop ——

He stopped short and bent horrified gaze on a bearded old man sitting with chair tilted back in front of one of the shops.

This old man was worse off than he was.

He didn't have *any leg at all!*

Where the old man's leg should have been was just a stump all covered with patches of cloth. Leaning up against the front of the shop beside the chair was a big, funny-looking peg with straps to it. As Eddie studied it and the man, he decided that whenever the man wanted to walk he had to strap the peg where the leg should have been.

" Hello, comrade! " the man called out cheerily.

Abashed at being observed, but encouraged by the friendly greeting, Eddie moved closer and gravely and silently inspected the man and his surroundings. The man must be very, very old, he decided, for he had long white whiskers. The shop looked old, too, and over the door was a blurred sign which read " JONAS TUCKER: Tobacco, Cigars, and Candies."

" Didn't you ever have any leg? " Eddie blurted out.

He felt he was being impolite in asking about it.   He knew how he was mortified when people asked him questions about his leg.   But something way down inside him insisted that he must know how it was to go through life without any leg at all.

Old Jonas chuckled merrily.   The boy looked on aghast.   How could a man without any leg ever laugh?

" Didn't you ever have any leg at all? " he repeated.

" It's fifty years this summer," the old man chuckled, " but, lordy, it was worth it!   I'd gladly lose the other leg to go through it all again."

Wide-eyed with interest the weary youngster sank down beside the old shopkeeper's chair, and soon was hearing the thrilling story of Gettysburg told by one who had fought there, by a veteran whose memories had just been delightfully refreshed by meeting on the battle-field again with his comrades of a half-century ago, and living over again the thrilling moments of Pickett's charge.   Interesting as Edward Haverford Randall had found the reading of war history, he found this narrative of a participant, of a soldier who had been

wounded there, vastly more absorbing. Spellbound he listened for a full hour, and when the
narrative was ended he delighted the veteran
with questions that showed familiarity with the
episodes of Gettysburg. His curiosity about
the battle at last sated, he began to ply his en-
tertainer with questions about life without a
leg.

He was amazed to find that Jonas belittled
his infirmity, optimistically asserting that you
could have just as much fun with one leg as
with two, and gallantly declaring that you were
even better off, for if you broke your wooden
leg it didn't hurt.

" And I see there's two of us," old Jonas
chuckled. " You haven't much of a leg yourself."

Somehow it did not mortify him in the least
to have the one-legged man talk about his
lameness. Instinctively he realized that old
Jonas must understand. Here was some one
to whom he could talk. Soon he was telling the
whole sad story of the afternoon — how the
boys would not let him play battle, how his
mother had been discussing him with a stranger,
how his father had said he was too lame to go on
the " hike," and about the little girl next door.

"Pooh, pooh," the old man advised him. "You mustn't mind them at all. I've been through it all, and I know. It isn't the shape of your body that counts. There's Napoleon, a pot-bellied dwarf, and look what he did. And Alexander Pope was a hunchback, but he held his own against all London. John Milton had no eyes, but they're still reading the poetry he wrote. Lord Byron was a clubfoot, but two countries are proud of him. You could go on naming them till your tongue was tired, the crippled and the handicapped that have done big things. There's the great Emperor William, in our own time, with an arm that's no good, and Helen Keller that can neither see nor hear. I tell you, boy, it ain't the shape of the body that counts, it's the shape of the soul."

"But," protested Eddie with conviction, "your soul hasn't any shape."

He knew about your soul. It was what went out of you when you died. If you had been good and belonged to church it went to heaven. A soul was something like smoke — only thinner, so thin you couldn't see it.

"You can't see people's souls," he announced decisively.

"Oh, yes, you can," old Jonas affirmed. "Everybody can't but we can. People like us whose legs aren't much good, who have to do a lot of sitting all by ourselves, we can see people's souls. Maybe your father and your mother and your brothers can't. They're stirring around too much. But people like you and me that have time to sit and watch, we get by and by so we can see people's souls."

"Can you see mine?" asked Eddie, awed.

"Sure I can," old Jonas asserted.

"What's it like?"

"A fine, straight, upstanding one it was till this afternoon, when you got to thinking a lot of bad thoughts. That bent it considerable. As I see it now it's all over to one side. Maybe you can get it straightened out again if you'll try to remember all the kind things your mother does for you, and how nice your dad is to you. And that Sweeney boy — what name did you say —?"

"Froggie."

"You've got to quit envying that big lummax of a Froggie Sweeney that doesn't know half as much as you do. What if he can run faster than you?—he doesn't know anything about Gettysburg. Which would you rather be, lame in the leg, or lame in the head like he is?"

"I'd rather not be lame in the head," said Eddie very soberly, as he began to realize the possibility of there being worse things the matter with you than a leg in braces.

"And now, young man," said Jonas, "you'd better be getting home or you'll be bending your soul some more by being late for supper."

"That's right," said Eddie, getting up with a start as he noticed how near sunset it was. "Good-by, and thank you very much."

"Good-by," old Jonas called after him. "And remember, don't mind what folks say about your leg. Just you sit and watch, and pretty soon you'll be able to see people's souls and tell what shape they are."

"Why, Eddie dear, where have you been?" Mrs. Randall asked anxiously as he took his seat at the table where the rest of the family had long been gathered. "Mother has been worrying about her boy."

She brushed back his hair with a little gesture of affection as she spoke, surreptitiously feeling his forehead, for the feverish excitement in his eyes as he entered had made her fearful of approaching illness. As always with mothers, her little lame chick was the one nearest her heart.

The touch of her cool hand and the loving kindness in her tones brought a great lump to the throat of the poor, tired, overwrought child. A wave of shame sent the color to his cheeks. To think that he ever could have doubted her, or questioned her affection for him!

"Just down street," he answered her. It was all he could manage to say. He wanted to tell her, to tell all of them, about the wonderful old man he had discovered who hadn't any leg at all, who could see people's souls. It was on his lips to speak, yet a dread of ridicule — a vague fear that they might not understand because they did not sit still enough — held him back, and, wise mother that she was, Mrs. Randall read in his face something that forbade further questions.

"Here, young man," his dad called out, " is a walker for you."

New turmoil started in the boy's repentant heart at this announcement. Both his brothers liked the leg of the chicken. It was a family joke that the farmers ought to raise three-legged chickens for the Randalls. All of a sudden it came to Eddie that Dad always saved a leg for him, even when he was late, making the other boys take turn about. Dad must love him almost as much as Mother did.

"Say, Ed," Tom announced in affectionate tones, "the stamps came — dandy ones. We'll look them over after supper, and divide. Dick doesn't want any, so you can have half."

Too choked for utterance, Eddie beamed his thanks. His oldest brother a few days before, with money earned cutting a neighbor's grass, had answered an advertisement, "800 foreign stamps, all different, for twenty-five cents." Eddie had just started an album, and as his opportunities for earning spending money were less than those of his brothers, had felt discouraged at his slow progress. He had never dreamed of such munificence as this. The best he had hoped for was that a few discarded duplicates might fall to his lot.

With heart full and eyes swimming he busied himself with his plate. How good they all were to him! What beautiful shapes their souls must have. Shyly he studied each one of them in turn. He wished he knew where to look. He wondered in what part of a person's body the soul was. He must ask the one-legged man the next time he saw him. He al-

always had thought of a person's soul as being
in their head, somewhere back of the eyes.
Maybe, though, it was down where your heart
is. He was sure there was nothing in the
physiology about it. He wished he knew for
certain.

Even though the conversation turned on tomorrow's hike, he was too grateful to resent being left out of it.   And then, to cap the climax,
he heard Richard saying:

" Out there by Bear Pond I know where
there's a lot of sassafras growing. I'm going
to take an old kitchen knife along and dig a lot
of roots, and bring them home to you, Eddie."

Oh, how good they all were to him! They
were always thinking of nice things to do for
him.   How could he ever have been so ungrate-
ful? No wonder the one-legged man said his
soul was bent. Mechanically he reached out
his hand to the biscuit plate.

" Wait a minute, Eddie," Maggie, the cook,
called out from the pantry door. "I've got a
couple I was keeping hot for you out in the
kitchen."

Even Maggie, black Maggie, was nice to
him! He wondered what her soul looked like.
Did black people have black souls? It must

be a nice shape, he decided, even if it was black. He eyed her solemnly and thoughtfully as she handed him the biscuit, pondering over the problem, although in his new mood of gratitude toward all the world he remembered to say, " Thank you."

All the rest of the evening, even when engaged in the absorbing occupation of dividing the stamps, he kept studying the family. He could not discover anything about any of them that looked like a soul. If only he had asked the one-legged man where to look. Perhaps mother would know. He waited until bedtime came to ask her. Always after he had unstrapped his brace and had put on his nightie, mother would come into his room. With cool, skillful fingers, she would massage his poor aching leg till all the dreadful pain from the iron that clamped it had vanished. Tonight as she bent over him he began to remember all the kind things she did for him — in fact for all of them. She never forgot how he liked his oatmeal, the cream first and then the sugar —" so you could see it." It was she who brought him interesting books from the library. It was she who gave him dimes for doing little household tasks with which his lameness did not interfere, thereby enabling him to compete with his more active brothers who were always earning money somehow. It was she who mended his clothes, who tied his necktie, who rubbed his leg every night, who made the desserts he liked, who helped him plan games that he could play by himself when he had to rest. It was she who doctored his bruises when he stumbled and fell —and that, poor chap, was several times a day. Mother, he thought, must have a wonderfully beautiful soul. It must be round, just like a shiny gold piece. How he did wish he could see the shape of mother's soul.

"Mother," he asked, "where is your soul?"

"Why, you funny boy!" she answered. "It's inside of you, of course."

"Yes, but where?"

Mrs. Randall was puzzled for a reply. This small son of hers often asked her questions that were hard to answer.

"You can not see the soul," she said finally, "so no one knows just where it is."

"Oh, yes, you can," Eddie affirmed. "Some people can see people's souls."

Accustomed ordinarily to accept his mother's word as final, the boy suddenly recalled what the one-legged man had said. Seeing souls was

a gift that came to people who had to sit still —
" to people like us." Mother was occupied all
day long doing so many things for all of them.
She never had time to sit still and watch.
Poor, busy, kind mother probably never had
had a chance to see people's souls. Maybe it
would not be nice of him to ask her any more
about it. She might not understand.

He lay so silent that his mother thought he
had fallen asleep. Pressing a soft kiss on his
forehead she tiptoed away, leaving him to lie
awake in the darkness, wondering what was the
shape of her soul, and wishing he could see it.
And somewhere on the borderland of sleep —
he remembered it so vaguely the next morning
he feared it might have been only a dream — he
had a vision of his mother bending over him,
and all around her head, making a wonderful
light in her eyes, was a great golden halo that
he knew must be her soul.

" Oh, mother, mother, I can see it," he was
sure he had cried out, but maybe he only
dreamed he had spoken.

" You can't imagine what Eddie asked me tonight," Mrs. Randall said as she joined her husband. " He wanted to know in what part of
your body your soul is."

"Kids get funny notions," said Mr. Randall carelessly. "I hope it doesn't rain tomorrow."

As a matter of fact, he was thinking neither about Eddie's question nor about the weather. Something far more important was occupying his mind. He had been debating whether or not to tell his wife about it, and while she was upstairs he had reached the conclusion that it would be better to keep it from her until it was settled.

It was an old, old problem he was facing. His practise as a lawyer gave him an income that was barely enough to feed and clothe and shelter his family. Mixing in politics in the hope of expanding his opportunities, he had been elected a councilman on a reform ticket. Close on the heels of his election had come an invitation to become one of the attorneys of the principal railroad that passed through the town. One of the planks in the platform on which he had run had been a demand for the abolition of grade crossings. The reason the position had been offered to him was as plain as two times two. "Yet," he was arguing with himself, "as counsel for the railroad I probably can do more toward abolishing grade crossings than otherwise.   I can fight better from within than from without.   Besides, a man's first duty is to his family.   I give my services to the city and am under no obligation to refuse four thousand a year."

Four thousand a year!   That, in addition to his present earnings, would enable them to live much more comfortably.   It would make it possible to send the boys to a good school, and later to college.   He could even afford to buy his wife an automobile.   Certainly she was entitled to it after all these weary years she had had of struggling to make ends meet.   There had not been much pleasure in her life with those three boys to take care of.   Yes, it was his duty to try to make things easier for her. Bother the ethics of the matter!   Other men in public life did similar things and much more flagrant things, and got away with it.   Why shouldn't he?

Then there was Eddie, poor little chap! With this addition to their income they could take him to see that great New York doctor who was making such marvelous cures of cases just like Eddie's.   It would be worse than wrong to let the boy go limping through life if a cure could be effected.   He must get the money to give Eddie his chance, and get it he would.

But potent as were these arguments a conscience begot of ten generations of Presbyterian ancestors, and fortified by fifteen years of happy marriage with a good woman — good all through — gave Randall no peace.

" At any rate," he consoled himself, " I don't have to give my answer until next Friday. It'll be time enough to tell her then."

If Mrs. Randall heretofore had been a woman of many cares, from this time on she had double worry. Her motherly intuition told her that two of her boys — the oldest, as she was accustomed to call her husband — and Eddie, both had something on their minds and both were keeping it from her, a most unusual proceeding. Several times she tried to draw Randall out, but he rejected her invitations to make a confidante of her.

And Eddie worried her still more. He seemed to have given up all hope of playing with the other boys. Day after day she found him sitting silent on the floor, his gaze fixed intently on her, or on some other member of the family. At times she heard him talking aloud to himself. She could not hear what he was saying although she thought it was something about "a round one." He had developed the habit of being mysteriously missing for two or three hours at a time. All she could get out of him when she questioned him as to where he had been was the same answer, "Just down street."

Yet the little lame boy never suspected for a moment that he was causing his mother any anxiety. He was wholly absorbed in the new game he was learning, endeavoring to see people's souls. Each day he managed to pay a visit to the one-legged man; they had become fast friends.

"It's no use," he said despondently to old Jonas. "I've tried and tried, and I never can see anything."

"Keep on trying," responded the old philosopher.

"How long?"

"How long did it take you to learn to read? I'll venture you was a good part of a year learning that, or maybe two years. T'ain't hard to learn to read, is it? Any one can do that. There's only a few of us that can see people's souls — folks like you and me, that have to sit still a lot — and naturally it's hard to

learn how to do it, but keep at it and some day
it will come to you just like that. Have you
never seen nothing at all with all your looking?"

"I think," said Eddie gravely, "that one
night I saw my mother's soul. Maybe I
dreamed it. It was a shiny golden circle all
around her head."

"It was no dream," old Jonas affirmed solemnly. "I'll warrant you really saw it.
That's what mothers' souls are like, all round
and golden and shiny. And it's little lame
boys like you that sees them best. You've seen
your mother's soul for sure."

The more Eddie thought about it the more
firmly he became convinced that he really had
seen the shape of mother's soul. But what
was his father's like, and those of his two
brothers? As he studied Tom and Dick he
came to the conclusion that theirs must be something like his own, nice straight ones, but apt
to get bent out of shape every now and then;
but the shape of father's soul was a puzzle. It
was a fascinating subject, and every evening
after father came home, until bedtime, Eddie's
eyes hardly left his father's face.

"Have you noticed anything strange about

Eddie?" Mrs. Randall asked her husband one evening after the boys were in bed, her voice almost breaking with anxiety.

"Why, no. What's the matter with him?"

"I can't find out. He just sits around all day staring at people, and sometimes talking aloud to himself. You don't suppose that his — lameness — and his suffering — could — could — be affecting his mind."

"Don't be silly! Of course not," Mr. Randall reassured her.

Randall was busy just then with his own problem. Brace, the head counsel of the railroad, had phoned that he would be out to see him tomorrow to learn his decision. He had suggested making the appointment at Randall's home.

"It's just as well not to have our meeting attract any attention," Brace had said, and Randall had assented, even though he recognized at once the sinister significance of not making their meeting too public.

He realized that this was his last opportunity to consult his wife before making his decision. While he kept telling himself that he had not yet made up his mind, he knew he was going to accept. Four thousand a year more meant so much to all of them! He was doing it, he told himself, to provide the funds to get Eddie's leg cured. Weren't his wife's happiness and his boy's health above all other considerations? What was the use of bothering his wife about it until it was settled? She was worried now about Eddie. Why worry her more?

" I'll be home about four tomorrow afternoon," he said. " I'm going to meet a Mr. Brace here."

" Is that so? " replied Mrs. Randall absently. She was thinking about her little lame boy, and hardly heard what her husband said.

Randall smoked on in silence, half hoping, half fearing that she would question him about Brace; but nothing further was said.

Eddie happened to be on the porch when his father arrived home the next afternoon, and recalling his wife's anxiety, Randall studied his son with unusual interest, and asked him questions, observing with some relief that the boy's intelligent answers gave no evidence of mental perturbation. In the midst of their conversation an automobile stopped at the gate.

" Now run away, son," he said, " here comes

a man with whom Dad has some business to talk."

With no thought of being an eavesdropper, Eddie didn't run away. He settled himself down on a hassock behind a porch chair. Here was an opportunity not to be neglected. He seldom had a chance to observe Dad while he was talking business. Perhaps it would be a good time to see his soul. He settled himself to watch, as his father and the visitor seated themselves.

He did not listen to the conversation. He would not have understood it if he had. With the clear vision of childhood, however, he sensed that the man was urging Dad to do something that Dad didn't want to do. As the boy studied the visitor's face something told him that this man had an ugly soul. He strained his eyes trying to see it, and failing, turned once more to study his father's face. Perhaps it was only that his sight was blurred from his strained staring in the sunlight, but he was certain he saw a vapory halo about his father's head, saw it losing its circular shape and beginning to send out angry, distorted tongues that twisted this way and that. Some unrestrainable impulse sent him scrambling to his feet. " Oh, Dad! " he shrilled, " your soul's all crooked! "

Just what happened after that he never could quite remember. He knew that both men had sprung to their feet. Dad had shouted " No! " in the man's face, and the man had gone away, and he found himself gathered into Dad's arms in a big, comfy chair on the porch. He had found himself explaining it all to Dad, how the one-legged man had said that people who had to sit still a lot by and by got so that they could see people's souls, and how he had tried to see if he could. He had seen mother's, and it was round and golden and beautiful. He had been trying and trying, he explained, to see Dad's, and he never had been able to until then when Dad and the man were talking.

" And it is true, Dad," he concluded; " you can see people's souls if you look for them."

" It certainly is, son, but, please God, you'll never see mine crooked again! "

But even to those who have the gift of see-ing souls there remains much mystery in life. Eddie doesn't understand yet why mother wept that night as she rubbed his leg.

He asked her, and she said it was because two of her boys had made her so happy that eve-

ning.   But if she was happy why did she weep?
It was too big a problem for Eddie.

"I'll ask the one-legged man about it tomorrow," he said to himself as he fell asleep.

CHAPTER TWO

MAINLY ABOUT WOMEN

IT lacked half an hour of school-time. The three Randall boys, Tom, Richard, and Eddie, always looking more spick and span at this time than during the rest of the day, sprawled in easy if ungraceful attitudes on the front porch steps, were discussing a portentous event in boydom of the day before.

"'Course," said Tom decisively, "there's times when a feller's just got to fight."

"Sure," Richard corroborated, "lots of times."

"You'd never fight, though, would you, Tom?" queried Eddie.

"You can just betcher life I would," Tom asserted.

"And me, too," echoed Richard.

Wide-eyed with wonder, little Edward Haverford Randall listened to his brothers' astounding declaration. Time after time he had heard both of them promise their mother that they never would fight. She had not asked

Eddie for a similar promise.   He was different
from other boys.   " It " made the difference, a
poor, undeveloped leg that required a cruel iron
brace to support it, a lame leg that kept him
from running and jumping and swimming as
other boys did, a hideous, ever-present grief
that was responsible for all the boys of his acquaintance, all but his own brothers, calling him
ever by the unwelcome name of " Limpy."
Even Tom and Richard sometimes forgot and
let the hated nickname slip out before they
thought.   Eddie knew, of course, that they
never did it on purpose, and he always tried to
pretend that he did not mind it in the least, especially since old Jonas Tucker had expounded
his theory that the shape of people's bodies
didn't matter, as it was only the shape of their
souls that counted.

"What's a feller going to do," Tom continued, "when another feller dares him? A
feller can't take a dare unless he's a coward."

"'T'sright," assented Richard. "And if he
calls your mother a nasty name, what's a feller
going to do?   He's just *got* to fight."

"But," protested Eddie, "you both promised mother you never would fight. I heard
you promise."

" Aw, forget it," said Tom. " Women don't understand things."

" 'T'sright," said Richard. " There's lots of things women don't know nothing about. When they ask you to promise, it's always best to say yes to keep them from worrying. You never hear Dad asking a fellow not to fight."

" I'll bet he had lots and lots of fights when he was a kid," added Tom. " I heard him and S. T. Elwell talking about a fight they had at school. They didn't know I was listening. It must 'a' been some scrap to hear them tell it."

From far down the street came a familiar sound, " Wheep-hu-hu-hu-wheep-hu-hu! "

It was the whistled call of the Randall boys' gang. It meant that Four-eyed Smith, or Fatty Bullen, or Froggie Sweeney had left his domicile and was in search of congenial company to while away the moments before the school-bell rang.

With an answering " Wheep-hu-hu-hu-wheep-hu-hu," Tom and Richard scrambled to their feet and dashed off.

Eddie, left all alone, as often happened, began to hobble slowly off toward school. Though it took him twice as long as it took the other boys to walk the four blocks, he never was

late.   Tom and Richard, no matter from where
or how soon they started, always seemed to arrive on the last tap of the bell — sometimes a
moment or two after it.   Eddie had never been
marked tardy in his life.   School was one of his
greatest pleasures.   In the class-room, at least,
he could compete with his fellows on equal
terms.   There, his crippled leg didn't matter.

On this particular morning, Eddie's mind
was busy with a new train of thought.   His
brothers' boldly proclaimed heresy that women
didn't understand things seemed to him revo-
lutionary, unbelievable, impossible.   Hitherto
he always had felt that mother understood
everything about everything.   Yet now, as he
began to ponder over the matter, he did not feel
quite so sure.   He recalled that when he had
tried to explain to her old Jonas's theories
about the shape of people's souls, she had not
seemed inclined to take much stock in them.
Still, Eddie, down in his heart, felt positive
that old Jonas was right.   Perhaps women
didn't always understand things.

The seeds of doubt sown by his brothers' remarks began to take root.   The boy began
nibbling for the first time at the fruit of the
tree of knowledge.   Even though it made him

feel vaguely unhappy, he kept on trying to analyze his world in this new aspect. Mothers, he knew from experience, understood what boys liked to eat. Mothers understood how to bandage cut fingers and to massage tired legs. Still, he could not help remembering that he often had heard mother, his own dear kind mother, say, " You'd better ask father."

He could not recall that she ever had said it to him. It must have been to his brothers that she had used the words. He racked his brains trying to remember what she had said it about. It must have been about something she did not understand. What was it? He wished he could remember.

He thought, too, about Miss Lizzie McGuffey, his teacher. Could it be possible that there were some things she didn't understand? He eyed her curiously as he entered the schoolroom, for here, at least in one respect, he was a privileged character. He never had to wait and march in with the others. On account of his lameness, he was permitted to enter whenever he arrived.

Often in these few minutes before school he and Miss McGuffey had delightful little chats. Ordinarily timid and shy in the presence of others, Eddie, when alone with her, asked her questions about things not made quite clear to him in class. Surely Miss McGuffey must understand everything. She never had failed him.

As Eddie entered, the teacher was busy at her desk and beyond a cheery " Good morning, Eddie," she did not seem disposed to talk. Just as well pleased, for he was still busy pondering over his freshly gained aspect of life, the boy made his way to his seat and rested there thoughtfully, solemnly eying Miss McGuffey and wondering if there really was anything she didn't know or didn't understand. Little could he suspect that at that very moment his goddess of knowledge was busily cramming up on the day's geography lesson.

Soon the other pupils filed in, and the day's routine began. It was one of those everdreaded trouble-days every teacher learns to expect occasionally. Perhaps it was because Miss McGuffey had been up late the night before, and the youngsters subconsciously recognized her panicky state of unpreparedness; perhaps it was because the backs of the seats were not scientifically curved. It may have been the order of the school board preventing the opening of the windows, except at recreation time, before April twentieth. It may have been due to the innate devilishness that at times seems suddenly to possess boydom, but, certainly, the pupils had hardly seated themselves before a subtle whisper of disorder swept over the room. Whenever Miss McGuffey's back was turned, notes and paper-wads went flying about. Even the star good-conduct pupils were caught whispering. None of them seemed to know their lessons. Miss McGuffey's nerves went to pieces, making her extraordinarily irritable and curt.

The climax came shortly before the noon recess. The " B " geography class was called. All the members filed up to their places except Froggie Sweeney. He had not far to go, for Miss McGuffey, for purposes of easy observation, had given him a seat well toward the front of the room. With all the others astir, Froggie sat sullenly in his seat.

" Sweeney," said Miss McGuffey sharply, " take your place."

The boy did not answer her nor make the slightest motion to indicate that he intended to obey.

"Sweeney," she repeated, still more sharply, "take your place at once!"

Still the boy made no movement.

Boys are not given to self-analysis. If Froggie had been asked to explain his stubbornness, it is doubtful if he could have done so. Let us be charitable and say that under the youngster's unprepossessing exterior and rough manners was concealed a sensitive soul, a timid spirit that shrank from and resented the ridicule that too often fell to his lot when he didn't know his lessons. Probably psychology would have found some such logical explanation as this. All that Froggie knew about it was that he had decided "he wasn't a-goin' to," and, having decided, he proposed to stick to it.

Her patience already tried beyond endurance, Miss McGuffey let pass from her mind all she had read on the necessity of gentleness in dealing with recalcitrant pupils. She decided that the terrible Sweeney boy needed dire punishment, and needed it immediately.

"Randall," she called out, "go to the principal's room and ask him to come here."

Ordinarily such a threat was sufficient to make the most mischievous boy behave. She half expected that before the messenger was despatched Froggie would be pleading for mercy. As it happened, Eddie did not at first realize that she was speaking to him. His mind was busy just at the moment with the commercial products of China, assuring himself that he still remembered the lesson studied the night before.

"Eddie!" she called out, this time in tones more curt and commanding.

The boy came to himself and stared at her uncomprehendingly. "Yes'm?" he said.

"Go and tell the principal to come here at once!"

"Yes'm," repeated Eddie obediently, starting at once to do his errand. But, even as he hobbled off, it came to him that it hardly seemed fair to make him a participant in another boy's punishment. Often before, Miss McGuffey had sent him on errands, but always of some pleasant nature. This was different. "Sending for the principal" was the worst punishment permissible. A teacher might set a bad boy to extra lessons, she might keep him in after school, she might mark him "D" in conduct, but beyond this she might not go. "Sending for the principal" invariably resulted in one of

three things, a letter home, a thrashing, or a
suspension—sometimes all three.

It seemed to Eddie wrong to involve him in
the trouble between Miss McGuffey and Froggie Sweeney. Going to summon the principal
seemed, somehow, to partake of "tattling."
He wished that he did not have to go. Yet
there was his own good-conduct record to be
considered. If he should refuse to go, undoubtedly the teacher would punish him, too.
He thought of trying to explain to her his
feelings about the matter, but, after one glance
at her flushed, angry face, he decided it would
be useless. It must be that his brothers were
right, that women didn't always understand
things.

He started for the door to carry out his mis-
sion. As he passed the desk at which Froggie
sat, sullen and glowering, head down and hands
in pockets, a shrill whisper reached him:

"I'll git you for this after school. I'll git
you, Limpy. See if I don't."

It was a terrified little cripple who made his
way to Professor Phillips's room and timidly
knocked. It was all he could do to find voice
to deliver his message. He was in such a panic
of fright that he hardly knew how he found his

way back to the schoolroom and to his place in
the class.   Even the spectacle of Froggie, still
sullen and defiant, being dragged from the
room by the muscular principal seemed only
a confused memory.

Eddie, hitherto protected by his weakness,
now for the first time in his life had been threatened with physical violence.   However remiss
Froggie might be in his attention to school
duties, in the world outside he had a far different reputation.   When Froggie Sweeney
announced his intention of " gittin' " a fellow,
the fellow was " got."   Froggie's pugilistic
abilities and achievements were the envy of his
mates.

Often and often Eddie had heard the matter
discussed by his admiring brothers.   There
was no doubt in his mind as to the meaning of
Froggie's threat.   Froggie intended to " lick "
him.   What should he do about it?

It was a terribly perplexing problem that
confronted him.   Suppose Froggie found him,
and he tried to run away?   Froggie would
quickly overtake him.   Suppose he tried to give
battle?   What chance had he against a boy
head and shoulders taller, and experienced in
fighting.   And, besides, his mother disap-

proved of boys' fighting.   Even if he did try to fight back, how grieved she would be with him! And, besides and beyond all this, he was afraid, afraid of being struck and pommeled.   The very thought of it sickened him.   Never in all his life had any one struck him or whipped him.

As he left the schoolroom at the noon recess, he was trembling with fear, shuddering at the thought of the peril that he faced on the journey home.

"What's the matter, Eddie, are you ill?" Miss McGuffey called after him as she caught a glimpse of his white, troubled face.

"Nothing," he stammered bravely.   Whatever happened, he would not tell her.   He felt that she wouldn't understand.   Down in his heart, too, he had still another vague, hardly realized sensation — a feeling that, somehow, Froggie had almost the right to punish him.

Still, the prospect of going home alone appalled him.   He thought at first of seeking the protection of his brothers.   Tom and Richard, he knew, would not let any one hurt him. With some idea of invoking their aid as allies, he waited until the pupils from their respective rooms came trooping out.   His brothers passed close by him, but something sealed his

lips. Without a word to them he watched
them scamper off with their mates. Perhaps it
was that in his mind there dwelt some of the
boydom talk he had so often heard about " no
feller ought ever to be a coward and a quitter."
Perhaps it was that in his trembling body there
resided a far more valiant soul than ever its
possessor suspected.

After nearly all the boys had vanished, Eddie set out for home. Froggie was nowhere to
be seen. From scraps of conversation, Eddie
gathered that the defiant pupil had " got licked
and got sent home, too." Whatever had happened, he felt sure that Froggie would keep his
word and would be waiting to waylay him.

He had passed two blocks in safety with no
signs of the enemy. Home was now only a little distance away. A short cut through Mc-
Millan's Alley and one more block, and he
would be safe in his own yard. He began to
breathe more freely. He felt that he was almost safe. But, as he turned into the alley, his
heart sank, and his mouth became suddenly
dry.

There in the middle of the alley, where he
would be less likely to be observed from either
street, stood an irate, revengeful Froggie, hair

tousled and eyes still red as a result of his visit to the principal's room.

Terrified though he was, Eddie kept right on. What else was there to do? He thought of running, but what would be the use? Handicapped as he was by his crippled leg and heavy iron brace, Froggie would overtake him before he had gone five yards. He wanted to scream for help, but his mouth was so parched from fright he could not have uttered a sound even if he had tried to do so. Nearer and nearer he approached his foe, who stood there with fists doubled up, aggressively waiting for him. Not until he was within six feet of the other boy did Eddie stop.

Froggie at once bore down on him menacingly. "Now, Limpy, I got you," he snarled. "I told you I'd fix you, you teacher's pet, and I'm goin' to. I'll teach you to go runnin' to the principal to git him to come and lick me."

Reveling in the terrifying effect of his tirade on the shrinking little figure before him, Froggie continued with his flow of abuse, winding up with a nasty name — the name at which Brother Tom had declared "a feller has just *got* to fight."

Quick as a flash, Limpy drew from the book-strap he was carrying a brass-edged ruler, and, mustering all his strength, slashed with it at Froggie's cheek. The blow caught the bully unprepared. The sharp edge cut into the cheek, leaving a long, vicious gash. Froggie amazed at the unexpected turn of affairs had taken, scared at the sight of his own blood, never offered to hit back, but ran bawling out of the alley and disappeared.

Aghast at the dire effect of his blow, Eddie staggered about dizzily for a second and then collapsed utterly. For several minutes he lay on the soft turf of the alley, trembling all over, weak from the unusual exertion, and still frightened—oh, so frightened!

But no longer was he afraid of Froggie. The bubble of the young pugilist's prowess had been forever pricked so far as Eddie was concerned. No, it was not Froggie that he feared now. He was afraid for himself. He, Edward Haverford Randall, whose mother sternly disapproved of fighting, had been fighting. He, the star good-conduct pupil of his room, had fought with another boy and had laid his cheek open.

What would mother say to him? What

would she do to him?   Would she, could she,
ever forgive him?

And what if Froggie died?   That cut on
Froggie's cheek now seemed to Eddie to have
been a frightful one.   The blood had poured
out all over Froggie's clothes.   Some of it even
had discolored the grass there in the alley.   Eddie looked at the splotch, where a moment ago
Froggie had been standing, and shuddered.
Suppose the blow from the ruler had cut an
artery, and Froggie bled to death?   Most
likely he would be arrested for murder.   They
would come and take him away and lock him
up in prison, and by and by, maybe, they would
hang him.

With a depressing sense of blood-guilt
weighing down his soul, he painfully gathered
up his books and hobbled homeward.   He
felt all wobbly in his stomach, and his head
ached.   He was still trembling all over, but
was somewhat relieved, when he reached home,
to learn that mother was out — gone to Aunt
Kate's for the day.   His brothers, boylike, noticed nothing unusual in his appearance, but
Black Maggie, the cook, with kindly eyes always for the youngest of the flock, saw that he
was not himself.

" Eddie's stayin' home dis afternoon," she announced to Tom.

" Mother isn't here to write him an excuse," protested his brother.

" Oh, dat's all right, chile," said Maggie; " you see dat Miss McGuffin an' tell her Master Eddie ain't feelin' well, an' that Mis' Randall ain't home, an' it'll be all right."

A gleam of hope came to Eddie's troubled mind as his affairs were thus decided for him. If he did not have to go to school in the afternoon, it would give him an opportunity to slip away and see the old soldier before his mother arrived home, tell him the whole story, and ask for his advice.

He felt far too excited and upset to eat any luncheon, and, right afterward, Maggie made him lie down on the sofa in the dining-room and pulled down all the blinds. He lay there quietly until his brothers were off to school and Maggie had gone out into the back-yard to hang up the wash. Then, slipping quietly out of the house and keeping well out of her sight, he headed down the street and found old Jonas sitting, with chair tilted back, in front of his tobacco shop.

" Well, well," said old Jonas, as he ap-

proached, " what's this?   Eddie Randall playing hookey? "

"No — not exactly," the boy replied.
" You see, Maggie thought I was sick and made
me stay home from school."

" And wasn't you sick? "

" I didn't feel so very well."

"What's the matter — been trying to
smoke? "

" No.   I had been fighting."   Even Eddie
himself marveled at the thrill of pride he felt as
he made the announcement.

" You don't tell me," exclaimed old Jonas.
" And did ye lick or get licked? "

Thus encouraged, Eddie, starting from the
very beginning, told the old veteran the whole
story of his encounter with Froggie Sweeney,
winding up with the question, " Do you think
it was very wicked for me to hit him with the
ruler?"

" It certainly was not," pronounced old
Jonas.   " You done exactly right.   I only
wisht I'd been there to give him another one for
you."

" But supposing Froggie dies? "

" Humph! he won't die.   It takes more than
a cut on the cheek to kill a tough young nut

like Froggie Sweeney. Look at that and
that," said the old man, pointing to two great
scars, one on his head and one on his left hand.
" I got them both when I was a boy, and I'll
warrant they was worse cuts than you give
Froggie. You can see they didn't kill me."

" But," questioned Eddie, " what'll mother
say about it? She doesn't believe in boys'
fighting. She's made my brothers promise her
never to fight."

" Need you be telling her? "

" I always tell her everything."

" That's right," said Jonas, nodding his head
sagely; " always tell your mother everything.
It's a good way for a boy to go through life.
Still, you never can tell how women-folk will
take what you tell them. If I was you, I'd tell
my father first, and let him tell her if he sees
fit. You see, Eddie, women don't understand
things."

Eddie gasped, marveling at this confirmation
of his brothers' opinion.

" Women and men are different," old Jonas
went on. " A man's life is mostly made up
of fighting. He's got to fight to make a place
for himself in the world. He's got to fight his
own bad habits and bad thoughts. He's got

to fight the people that try to impose on him. If he hasn't learned how to fight and when to fight while he's still a boy, he's got a lot of lickings coming to him when he's growed up. There's lots of men makes failures in life because, as boys, they never learned how to fight.

"You see, Eddie, women don't know much about fighting. Most of them never have to do much of it. Their men, their fathers and brothers and husbands, yes, and sometimes their sons, too, do their fighting for them. The women-folk are the peacemakers of the world, the angels of mercy that bind up the wounds of the men-folk when they've been fighting. Women see only the brutality of fighting and the hurts it gives the ones they love, and few of them ever get the why of it. That's why women don't like fighting. Women don't understand things."

Strangely comforted by his talk with old Jonas, Eddie, as he went homeward, felt, nevertheless, that his world was falling to pieces. He had been so sure that his mother and Miss McGuffey knew everything about everything. Already he had put Miss McGuffey in the doubtful class. But wasn't mother still entitled to his full confidence? He felt, somehow, that he would just have to tell her about having fought Froggie.

And yet, if he did tell her, she would be so angry and so grieved with him. Perhaps she would never forgive him or trust him again. Probably she would cry. If he didn't tell her himself, there was little likelihood of her ever hearing about it. Tom and Richard, he was sure, never would tell on him. Should he or shouldn't he confess his crime? He could not make up his mind.

Reaching home before his mother, all afternoon and evening until bedtime he avoided her as much as he could, trying to attract as little attention to himself as possible. In answer to her questions about his illness, he said truthfully that he had had a headache, that Maggie had kept him home from school, had made him lie down, and that he felt all right now. The longer he put off his confession, the more determined he became not to make it. It would only worry and grieve his mother to know about it. What was the use of telling her? No, he decided, he would not tell her at all.

As he kissed his father good night and went up-stairs to bed, his mind was firmly made up. The longer he kept his secret, the easier it seemed to keep.   But, as he lay in his nightie, with mother's kind fingers massaging his aching leg, a sudden revulsion of feeling came over him.   He just must tell.   He couldn't keep anything from mother.   She was always so good, so kind to him.

"Mother," he blurted out, "I was fighting today."

"What!" she cried in astonishment.

"I was fighting today," he repeated, amazed to observe that she seemed more curious than angry.

"Tell mother about it, dear," she said softly.

Wondering that she still called him "dear," he told the story.   "Miss McGuffey sent me for the principal, 'cause Froggie Sweeney wouldn't go to class.   Froggie whispered that he'd get me after school, and he was waiting for me in McMillan's Alley as I was coming home. He was going to hit me, and I up and slashed at him with my ruler and cut his cheek open, and he ran away crying."

"Oh, my darling, brave, little boy," his mother cried, gathering him into her arms. "Mother's own little hero.   Tell me, Eddie dear, you are sure he didn't hit you or hurt you?"

"No'm," said Eddie. "I hit him before he had a chance to hit me."

"Oh, that horrid Sweeney boy!" she exclaimed. "You're quite sure he didn't hurt you? That Sweeney boy must be punished. I'm going right down-stairs and tell your father."

Eddie couldn't understand it at all. He had been so certain his mother would be angry at him and would scold him and would ask him to promise never to fight again! Yet here she was, calling him her darling and her hero, and it was Froggie she seemed to be angry at, not him. He could hear her now down-stairs, telling father how that brute of a Sweeney boy had attacked Eddie, and how Eddie, brave little Eddie, had so nobly defended himself. In his father's voice, too, as they discussed it, Eddie heard a note of pride. He could not understand it at all.

As he fell asleep, Eddie was still wondering. Didn't women understand things? He could not decide. Yet early next morning he found the answer. He was still dawdling over his breakfast in the dining-room. Dad had gone to business. Mother was up-stairs making up the beds, while Maggie finished the ironing.

Tom and Richard were on the front porch. Along came Froggie Sweeney.

"H'lo."

"H'lo, Froggie."

"Where's Limpy?" Eddie heard him ask.

"He's eating his breakfast."

"I got sompin for him."

Eddie abruptly left the table and hobbled to to the window, peering out from behind the sheltering curtains.

"What you got?" asked Tom curiously, wondering at this sudden friendliness.

"See this cut," said Froggie, pointing proudly to the mass of adhesive plaster on his cheek. "Limpy gave it to me. I brung him a flag of truce."

"How'd he do it? What is it?" asked Tom and Richard together.

"It's a flag of truce after the battle," grinned Froggie. "Me an' Limpy was fightin' yesterday, and, say, he's the gamest little kid you ever saw!"

"What," exclaimed Tom, "you and Limpy fighting!"

"Sure we was. I was layin' for him after school, pretendin' I was goin' to lick him for goin' for the principal, and he ups and hits me

with his ruler and cuts my cheek open. Ain't
he the game little kid, though?"

"He sure is," chorused his brothers.

To Eddie, listening, came a new sensation, a
great thrill of pride in himself. At last he had
made a place for himself in boydom. He was
one of them. Froggie Sweeney, Froggie the
fighter, had called him a game little kid. Life
took on a new and more joyous aspect.

"An' just to show there's no hard feelin's,"
Froggie went on, "I've brung Limpy one of
my pet white rabbits."

"Let's see it."

Once again Eddie's heart almost burst with
joy and pride. A pet white rabbit! Just the
very thing he had been longing for. And
Froggie had brought it over to give to him.
Oh, wasn't life grand and glorious! He just
must get out there on the porch quick to see it.
He must tell Froggie, too, that he had no hard
feelings, either.

He started for the door, but stopped abruptly, as he heard his mother's voice. She
had come down-stairs unobserved, and was
standing in the doorway, looking disparag-
ingly at the unsuspecting Froggie.

"You, Froggie Sweeney," she was saying

angrily, "you get right out of this yard, and don't you ever dare show your face here again. And take your rabbit with you. Eddie wouldn't have it. How dare you offer it to him after what you did to him yesterday? None of my boys ever want to have anything to do with you. No, you can't leave the rabbit. We don't want it. Get out of here!"

Edward Haverford Randall gulped down a great sigh of disappointment and went slowly back to finish his breakfast. He realized now that his brothers were right, that old Jonas was right. Women don't understand things.

CHAPTER THREE

GIVING AND GETTING

THE two of them, old Jonas Tucker, and Edward Haverford Randall, aged ten, sat, as they were generally to be found in the afternoon after school, before old Jonas's tobacco-shop. Jonas was tilted comfortably back in his chair, his leather stump unbuckled and propped up beside him close at hand. Eddie faced him from the top of an upturned dry-goods box. Ever since the first day of their acquaintance the boy had had the habit of coming to old Jonas with all his troubles. Somehow their mutual misfortune seemed to the boy to deepen and strengthen the understanding between them.

Eddie had just been complaining because his mother would not let him go off with his brothers on a fishing-trip the next day.

"You see," he explained, "it's only a mile or a mile and a half to Edlow's Pond, and I

can walk that far easy.   I've often walked that
far.   Mother said Tom and Richard could go,
but she wouldn't let me go."

"What do you s'pose she's keeping you
home for?" asked Jonas quizzically.   "Just to
be mean?"

"Oh, no!   It's nothing like that," Eddie replied quickly.   "I suppose she's afraid I'd get
tired or get hurt or something."

"Well, what of it?   Maybe there'll be more
fun in staying than going."

"I don't see how that could be."

"Well, you see," explained Jonas, "fun is
all in the way you look at things.   There's a
lot more happiness in giving than in getting;
yet most people are so busy trying to get things
for themselves that they never find it out."

"But don't you like to have people give you
things?"

"Yes and no," said old Jonas.   "Fact is,
I'd rather do the giving myself."

"How do you mean — giving?   I don't understand."

"You can't understand till you try it.   Did
you ever think how much other people give
you?   Your father and mother give you a
home, and lots of good things to eat, and

clothes to wear, and a nice bed to sleep in, and toys and things. Your teacher gives you an education. And what do you give them?"

"No-nothing," stammered Eddie thoughtfully. "I haven't anything to give."

"Don't you be so sure of that," Jonas asserted.

"What could I give any one?" queried Eddie, still dubious.

"Well, you've got yourself, for one thing. Now here's your mother that likes all of you boys and never sees much of you week days, because you're in school. Now, when Saturday comes, you all want to go fishing, and she wants one of you to stay at home. Just think how lonesome she'd be all day with you all away. You could give her yourself the whole day tomorrow."

"I never thought of that," Eddie confessed.

"Tell you what, Eddie, s'posing we call tomorrow a give day and just see how much you can give other people and see how it goes. Whenever you get a chance to give your services to any one, you just up and do it. Here you are, ten years old —"

"Nearly eleven," interrupted Eddie.

"Nearly eleven years old, and all these years

you've been getting without giving.   Try it
the other way 'round for a change."

"I'll do it," said Eddie with conviction.
"Tomorrow's going to be my give day — my
very first give day."

All the way home and all that evening he
was ransacking his brains for ways and means
of giving.   "What could he give to his father,
his mother, his brothers?"   The more he
thought about it, the more he realized how
heavy the balance stood against him.   All of
them were always giving him things.   What
had he ever given to any of them?

But what had he to give any of them?   After
supper that evening he went off upstairs to his
own room and overhauled the trunk in which
he kept his treasures.   He knew there was
nothing there that would be of much interest
to either his father or mother, but perhaps he
might find something that would appeal to
Tom or Richard.   In his enthusiasm over his
first "give day" he was determined that it
should include every member of the family.

As his brothers were going to make an early
start on their fishing-trip and were to be gone
all day, he decided he must find something for
them before he went to bed.   One by one he

went over his possessions. There was his
stamp-album. Both his brothers had albums
already, much more complete than his. Eddie's, in fact, was made up largely from the
specimens they had discarded as duplicates.
There were his beloved books. It would be
useless to offer them. Tom and Richard cared
little for books. No, there was nothing in the
trunk that would do for either of them. As
he put back the articles, he stood meditating
with his hands in his pockets. Instinctively
his fingers closed on his dearest possession, his
knife, the wonderful knife that Uncle George
had given him only a week before, with four
blades and a file and a screw-driver. Richard
wanted that, he knew. Hadn't he offered to
trade him all sorts of things for it? So far he
had refused all offers. He just couldn't give
up that wonderful knife. The more he
thought about it, the more he wanted to keep
it. All the blades in it were ever so sharp.
He wanted it, too, for carving out a boat. He
was going to begin just as soon as he succeeded
in finding the right kind of a piece of wood.
He must discover something else for Richard. He just couldn't get along without that
knife.

He was still racking his brains for some
other gift when bedtime came.   As his mother,
after unstrapping his brace, was massaging his
leg, as she always did, a new appreciation of
her kindness came to Eddie.   He felt that
every day was a "give day" with mother.
She was always giving up her time to do things
for him.

"Say, Mother —" he began.

"Yes, Eddie dear, what is it?" she asked,
quite accustomed to her youngest's bedtime
confidences.

"I'm glad I'm not going tomorrow.   I'd
rather stay here with you."

"I'm so glad," she answered.   "Mother
would be very lonesome with all her boys gone
all day."

"I don't mind a bit," said Eddie.   "It'll be
a lot of fun staying at home."

"You're a dear boy to say that," said Mrs.
Randall, giving him an extra hug as she bade
him good night.

An unwonted sense of peace and comfort
filled Eddie's soul.   Old Jonas was right; it
did make you feel good to say nice things and
do nice things.   And as Eddie fell asleep, he
had almost decided to give the knife to Richard.

But still there was Tom — what could he give Tom?

A breakfast-table conversation the next morning decided the question for him.

" Tom," said Mr. Randall sternly, " you promised that if I would let you go fishing to-day, you would cut the grass of the front lawn yesterday afternoon. Why didn't you do it? "

" I forgot," was Tom's truthful reply.

" I've half a mind not to let you go," said his father.

A gleam of pleased delight came to Eddie's face. Here was a chance to do something for Tom. " I'm not going today, Father," he said, " I'll cut the grass. It'll give me something to do."

In the look of surprise in his father's face at his unusual activity and in the expression of gratitude in his brother's countenance, Eddie felt well repaid.

" Well," said Mr. Randall, " I'll let Tom off this time as you agree to do it, but all you boys must keep your promises when you make them."

" Yes, sir, we will," answered Tom as the chief offender.

A little later, while lunch was being packed,

Eddie found a minute alone with Richard. "Say, Dick," he announced, "here's my knife you can have if you want it."

"What!" exclaimed his delighted brother, "you don't mean it!"

"Sure," said Eddie. "You can have it. I don't want it."

"You mean just for today or for keeps?"

"For keeps," said Eddie bravely.

"Gee, Eddie," said his brother, "that's great! I wish you was going with us. But never mind, I'll bring home a lot of willows for you, an' I'll show you how to cut a whistle."

In his satisfaction at the auspicious way in which his "give day" had begun, Eddie felt hardly a pang of disappointment as his brothers started off. As soon as they were out of sight, he got out the lawn-mower. He pretended he was an invading army. The grass was the enemy. Boldly and determinedly he fell to the attack. Even where the enemy made desperate resistance along the edge of the walk and under the shelter of the shrubs, it was quickly vanquished. Almost before he knew it, the task he had undertaken in his brother's behalf was done.

"It wasn't any work at all. It was just

fun," he said to himself as he put the lawn-mower away.

Made thirsty by his labors, he invaded the kitchen for a drink of water. Black Maggie, the cook, was out on the back porch shelling peas and grumbling.

" I don't see why we got to have peas on the day I's got ma sweepin' and dustin'," she complained.

Eddie's condition of self-satisfaction received a sudden and severe jolt. In his " give day " plans he had forgotten to include Maggie, and she did lots of nice things for him. She saved him hot rolls when he was late for meals. Often, too, she made the gingerbread and cookies he liked. Had he ever done anything for her? Had he ever given her anything? He could not remember that he had. Here was his opportunity. He could offer to shell the peas for her.

" Let me shell 'em," he suggested.

" Run away, chile," she ordered; " don't bother me."

" No, I mean it," Eddie persisted; " let me do them."

Amazed beyond further protest at such surprising and unusual consideration, Maggie relinquished the huge bowl of peas and with a doubtful shake of her head vanished to attend to her sweeping.   There on the porch, industriously splitting the never-ending supply of pods, Mrs. Randall found Eddie on her return from market.

" What's mother's boy doing? " she asked.

" Shelling the peas," he answered.

Unobserved by her son, Mrs. Randall opened her purse and then made a pretense of fumbling among the pods.   " My, what a lot you've got done," she said as she passed on into the house.

A few minutes later Eddie followed her with a delighted shout.   " Oh, Mother! " he cried, holding up a bright, shining dime. " Look what I found in the bottom of the pail of peas."

" Well! well! " exclaimed Mrs. Randall with well-simulated surprise.   " I wonder how that came there! "

" May I have it? " Eddie asked.

" Why, certainly!   Finders, keepers.   You deserve it surely for shelling all those peas."

" May I go and get an ice-cream with it? "

" You may do what you like with it; you found it," his mother said.

His heart aglow with all the sudden and newly acquired wealth, Eddie grabbed his cap and started down the street.

" I'll bet Tom and Richard aren't having any more fun than me," he soliloquized, more jubilantly than grammatically, thinking how much he would enjoy telling them about the finding of the mysterious dime among the peas, and of how surprised they would be. " I'll bet neither of them ever found any money like that. A give day's lots of fun."

Just then it came to him, with the thought of the " give day," that thus far he had given nothing to his mother — to mother, who gave him most of all. He slackened his pace and fell into deep thought. What could he give her? He had ten cents to spend as he liked. Why not, instead of buying something for himself, buy something for her? He felt sure that that was what old Jonas would advise. Yet what was there that he could get for ten cents that his mother would like? As if in answer to his question a sign loomed up before him on the florist's window, " Fresh Lilacs, Only Ten Cents a Bunch." But right next door was the ice-cream parlor.

Eddie was only human, and ice-cream to a

boy is always spelled in capital letters. He gazed for a moment into the florist's window. He could, to be sure, get an ice-cream soda for five cents. Perhaps he could prevail on the florist to split a bunch of lilacs and give him five cents' worth. Still he felt that such a compromise would not do. It was mother who gave him most of all. He would spend all his money for her.

His mind quickly made up, he went hurrying back home, carrying a great bunch of the fragrant blossoms.

"Home so soon?" his mother called out in surprise, as she heard his footsteps on the porch.

"Yes'm," cried Eddie, "and look what I've got for you." As he spoke, he plumped into her lap the armful of flowers, eying her expectantly to see if she liked them.

Only mothers, mothers delighted beyond measure at unexpected appreciation from those dearest to them, know how to say the words that brought a happy thrill to Eddie's heart, that filled his throat with a funny, choky feeling, and spread through his whole being a sense of peace and satiety that all the ice-cream in the world could not have produced. And while he and his mother sat there in one of those rare moments of complete understanding and appreciation, such as all too seldom come between mother and son, Mr. Randall entered, unexpectedly come home to luncheon. He was carrying all sorts of interesting-looking and mysterious packages.

"I don't know why those two lazy boys should have all the picnics in this family," he said exuberantly. "Just look what I've got here. Eddie, you open them."

A delighted shout from Eddie announced each new discovery. "Macaroons!" "Candy!" "Ice-cream!"

"Oh, good!" exclaimed Mrs. Randall. "We'll have a picnic all to ourselves out on the back porch — just the three of us. It's quite warm enough to eat outdoors."

"That'll be fine!" cried Mr. Randall.

"Great!" said Eddie.

"And Eddie's to have all the ice-cream he can eat," announced his mother. "He has earned it. He cut the grass, and he shelled the peas for Maggie, and with ten cents he found he bought me all these wonderful lilacs, the very first I've seen this year. See!"

"My, but they are pretty!" exclaimed Mr.

Randall in proper appreciation, as Eddie flushed with becoming pride. " And after the picnic we'll all go to the ' movies.' "

Late that afternoon, Eddie, tired out after the " movies," yet thoroughly happy in the consciousness of a day well spent, was swinging idly in the hammock on the front porch, wondering how soon his brothers would be back from their fishing-excursion. It did not seem possible that so many pleasant and interesting things could have happened in the same day — and to think that only yesterday he had looked forward with dread to being left at home! As he lay there, content in pleasant retrospection, an odd whirring noise reached his ears. It seemed to come from somewhere up in the sky. Eddie hastily scrambled out of the hammock and hobbled into the street to look up. At what he saw he gasped in amazement.

" It's an air-ship," he cried excitedly, as he saw a great birdlike thing moving rapidly toward him. Though it was the first aeroplane he or any one else in the town had seen, he recognized it at once from pictures.

As he looked, the whirring ceased, though the biplane glided on and on, coming nearer and nearer, and, oh, joy! coming down!

"Oh!" he cried. "It's going to stop here."

As fast as his lameness permitted, he headed for Tucker's back lot, arriving there before any one else, just as the great aeroplane settled slowly and gracefully down to earth. A leather-jacketed young man climbed out of the seat and pushed back his goggles.

"Here, young fellow," he said, extending his watch, "make a note of the time. I'm in the intercity race, and I've got to have a witnessed record of how long I stop. Where can I get some oil?"

"There's a garage just two blocks down the street," said Eddy, pointing excitedly; "down that way. Can I go for it?"

"I'll get it myself," said the aeronaut, striding rapidly away. "Watch her till I come back."

Eddie quickly found himself the center of an interested crowd eager to inspect the aeroplane, and he proudly explained to all of them about the race. As the aviator returned and began putting in the oil and tightening up the braces, a sudden daring resolve came to Eddie.

"Would you mind very much," he asked politely, his voice almost sinking away in his throat as he did so, " if I got my brother's camera and took a picture of you and your air-ship? "

" Go ahead," said the man, " I'll be here at least ten minutes longer."

In a jiffy Eddie was back with Tom's camera and tremblingly squeezed the bulb while the obliging aviator posed beside his ma-chine, and the crowd looked on enviously.

" Now, wait a minute," said the aviator as Eddie carefully turned the film.   Taking the camera from him, he lifted Eddie into the seat of the aeroplane and snapped a picture of him sitting there holding the wheel.

" There you are, kid," he said, returning the camera.   " Now you've got two pictures worth having.   And here, sign this record — twenty-two minutes for a stop.   You are the only one that was here when I landed."

Feeling more important than ever before in his life, Eddie, turning the precious camera over to his father to guard, grasped the avia-tor's fountain-pen and wrote his name — not, it must be confessed, in his best handwriting — but his full name, Edward Haverford Ran-dall.

A moment later the engine was started, the

propeller-blades began to revolve, the whirring
sound increased in volume, for a few yards the
great machine glided over the turf, and then,
rising slowly and gracefully above the fence,
above the houses, it mounted up and up and
sped farther and farther away until finally it
was lost in the distant sky, and the miracle was
over.

At supper that night Eddie and his father
were still discussing the wonderful event and
looking again and again at the pictures which
Mr. Randall had had the photographer de-
velop and print at once.

" You can tell it's me, can't you? "   Eddie
asked for about the tenth time, as the steps of
Tom and Richard were heard on the porch.
" Let me tell them about it," he whispered, and
his parents nodded assent.

" Well, boys, what luck? " asked Mr. Randall as they entered.

" We didn't get a bite," said Tom crossly.
" And I broke my new fishin'-rod."

" An' Eddie, all the blades in your knife got
broke," added Richard.

" I don't care," said Eddie, " if you broke a
hundred blades."

Something in his jubilant tone attracted the attention of both his brothers. " What's happened? " they asked, suddenly suspicious.

" Oh, nothing much," said Eddie, struggling to restrain his impatient tongue.

" Oh, go on, tell us," demanded his brothers, now reading something unusual in the faces of all three of the home-stayers.

" I cut the grass," began Eddie slowly, feeling that his narrative was entirely too exciting to tell all at once, " and then I shelled the peas, and what do you think?   I found ten cents in the pail."

" Is that all? " asked Richard disappointedly.

" No, that's not all," said Eddie triumphantly. " Dad came home to lunch with macaroons and candy and ice-cream, and we had a picnic on the back porch, and then Dad took us three to the movies —"

" Pooh! That's nothing," said Tom, although his face showed sad regret at having missed the fun.

" But wait! " shrilled Eddie, his voice rising in his excitement. " There was a great big aeroplane came sailing through the sky, and it came down and landed right in Tucker's back lot, and I was the very first person there when it got there, and the man asked me to watch it while he went and got some oil, and I watched it, didn't I, Dad? And then he let me take a picture of him and it with your camera, Tom, and then he took a picture of me sitting right in the aeroplane, and he got me to sign his report as an official witness; nobody else but me, didn't he, Dad? And here's the pictures we took."

Quickly his brothers grasped the photographs, even their hunger forgotten in their eagerness to see this confirmation of Eddie's wonderful tale.

" Oh, gee! " said Tom sadly, " I'd a lot rather 'a' stayed at home."

" Sure," said Eddie happily, " a give day is lots more fun than a fishing day."

In the excitement of looking at the photographs nobody noticed Eddie's remark except his mother — somehow mothers notice everything — and after supper, when Eddie had conducted his brothers out to Tucker's back lot to show them the exact spot where the aeroplane had landed, Mrs. Randall said to her husband:

" Wasn't Eddie a dear to spend all his

money for those lilacs for me, but he does say such queer things. I wonder what he meant by a ' give day '? "

" A what? " asked Mr. Randall, who was busy with the evening paper.

" A ' give day,' " Mrs. Randall repeated.

" I don't know," he replied carelessly. " Boys get funny notions."

So Mr. and Mrs. Randall never did know about their youngest son's first give day and how it turned out, but Eddie told old Jonas all about it the next afternoon.

" And you were right, Mr. Jonas," he concluded. " Giving is lots more fun than getting. I'm going to try to make every day a give day as long as ever I live."

Old Jonas nodded his head sagely. He didn't have to say anything. Eddie knew that he approved. It takes these lame fellows that have to sit around a lot to understand each other.

CHAPTER FOUR

PEACE WITH HONOR

"WHAT'S more," asserted Tom, "I'm not going to do it any longer."

"You dassent quit," said Richard. "There'll be a fuss if you do."

"I don't care."

Eddie did not say anything at all. He just sat there, an amazed and silent auditor.

"There isn't another boy I know as old as me," Tom continued, "who kisses his father good night."

"I'll bet Froggie Sweeney don't," said Richard with conviction.

"No, nor Four-eyed Smith."

"Nor Fatty Bullen."

"No, there's none of them do it, and I'm going to quit."

"I will if you will," said Richard.

"All right. We'll quit tonight."

"And what about Limpy?" Richard queried.

Eddie blushed painfully. Even if he did have to wear an iron brace on his leg, he did not like his brothers calling him by the resented nickname. It was bad enough when the other boys used it. True, it was seldom that his brothers forgot. Their lapses happened only when they were discussing some topic of absorbing interest.

"Limpy — Eddie can do as he likes," directed Tom loftily. "He is not old enough for it to make any difference to him. You and I are lots older and bigger than he is. The idea of a fellow of fourteen having to go around kissing people! I'm through with it."

"You're still going to kiss mother, aren't you, Tom?" questioned Eddie eagerly.

"I guess so," said his brother slowly; "that's different."

"Sure it's different," added Richard. "Women like kissing and being kissed. They never get over it."

"It goes then," asked Tom, "no kissing father tonight?"

"It goes, cross my heart and hope to die," said Richard.

"It goes," said Eddie solemnly after a mo-

ment's thought. He resented Tom's reference
to his youth. He did not like being considered
different from other boys. Personally, he had
not the slightest objection to kissing his father.
He could not understand why Tom objected
to it. Still he felt it was somehow up to him
to stand by his brothers.

The momentous question decided, nothing
more was said about it among the boys until
nine o'clock arrived that evening.

" Come, boys," said Mrs. Randall, " it's bedtime."

For once, for almost the first time in Randall history, there was no protest against having to retire so early. Tom and Richard
promptly got up to leave the room, exchang-
ing meaning glances as they did so. Eddie
sat undecided, timorously watching his more
daring brothers, as with heads erect they
marched out of the living-room.

" Boys," their mother called after them,
" you forgot to kiss your father good night."

Pretending not to hear, they began ascend-
ing the stairs. " Thomas, Richard," Mrs.
Randall called out sharply, " come back here
and kiss your father good night."

Mr. Randall, suddenly aware that something

out of the ordinary was happening, put aside his evening paper and looked up.

"I'm not going to kiss father any more," announced Tom boldly from the stairs. "I'm too old for kissing."

"Me, too," echoed Richard.

An amused smile crept over Mr. Randall's face. He recalled a somewhat similar revolt in his own boyhood. Into his wife's eyes, however, came tears of amazement and sorrow.

"Eddie, dear," she said appealingly, "come and kiss your father good night."

The little fellow's first impulse was to obey, but he remembered that his word was pledged to his brothers. What would they think of him if he did not keep the pact? "No'm," he said, "I'm not going to."

With that he hobbled bravely from the room, feeling a bit wobbly in his heart, almost wishing he had not promised, yet finding comfort in the thought that he was proving to Tom and Richard that he could be as game as they even if he was not as old.

Mrs. Randall looked with puzzled eyes after her youngest, and as soon as he was out of the room gave way again to tears.

"Never mind," said her husband soothingly,

"all boys get that kind of feelings. Don't bother about it."

"But Eddie, too," she sobbed; "he's always been such a good boy."

"Oh, boys are all alike," said Mr. Randall with assumed indifference. "Just let them alone. Now don't you go fussing and crying over them tonight."

"But," she cried piteously, "I can't understand what's got into them."

"It's just boy," said her husband understandingly. "Now let them alone. Don't go up-stairs and don't kiss one of them."

"Don't you think I'd better?" she asked anxiously. "Don't you think they want to kiss me, either?"

"Sure they do. Boys never outgrow a mother's kisses. They'd miss them more than you would. But if they want your kisses, make them come after them."

"But — but — I must go up and massage Eddie's leg," protested Mrs. Randall, and once up-stairs, regardless of her husband's advice, she gave each of her sons the customary good night kiss, to their surprise and relief saying nothing about the evening's unusual occurrences. The next night, too, the boys were permitted to go to bed without kissing their father, and no comment was made about it.

"It came easier than I thought it would," observed Tom to Richard.

"Sure," said Richard, "they didn't put up hardly any holler about it."

Only Eddie, of the three, felt vaguely dissatisfied and uneasy. Naturally affectionate in disposition, and perhaps somewhat spoiled and petted on account of his infirmity, he really had enjoyed the evidence of paternal affection; still even he had no intention of weakening in his resolve not to kiss Dad any more. The praise bestowed on him by his brothers for backing them up in their revolt had been far too much appreciated. "I didn't think Eddie had it in him," had been Richard's admiring comment.

"Sure he has," said Tom. "Eddie's as game a kid as they make."

Eddie's heart had swelled with pride at these tributes, little thinking that that very evening his gameness would be put to a further and still sterner test.

It was in the afternoon after school when he first realized that there was something in the wind. He saw his brothers and several of the other older boys whispering together excitedly about something. He hung around for a while, hoping vainly that they would take him into their confidence in recognition of his recent advancement in his brothers' estimation.

Seeing no signs of his being permitted to share in their secret, he finally gave up hope and went off by himself, spending the afternoon till supper time, as was his custom, chatting with his crony, old one-legged Jonas Tucker, in front of old Jonas's tobacco-shop. He did not see his brothers again until they were gathered at the table.

"Father," Tom was asking as Eddie took his seat, "can Richard and I go over to Fatty Bullen's for a little while this evening?"

Frequently the boys were allowed to go out after supper, if they asked permission, but tonight, to Mrs. Randall's surprise as well as to that of the boys, a different answer came.

"No," said Mr. Randall, "I want all you boys to stay in your own yard tonight."

"Aw, please, father," protested Richard, "can't we go for a little while?"

"I said ' No,' and I mean it," Mr. Randall answered in his sternest manner.

Two much depressed youngsters finished

their supper in silence, and as soon as they were through adjourned to the back yard, where an indignation meeting was held, with Eddie as an interested listener. "Did you ever hear of anything so mean?" exclaimed Tom. "He's always let us go before."

"He's doing it just to get square with us for not kissing him," affirmed Richard, viciously kicking at the turf.

"And to have to stay in tonight of all nights," groaned Tom.

"Why tonight?" asked Eddie. "What's going on?"

"Froggie Sweeney's sister's getting married tonight," explained Richard condescendingly, "and the fellers — the big fellers — are going to give them the grandest kind of a 'shivaree.'"

"What's a 'shivaree'?" asked the puzzled Eddie. He spent so much of his time reading that generally it was his brothers who asked him the meaning of words, but, as it happened, he had never run across any mention of the charivari in any of the books he had read.

"It's — well, anyhow," said Richard, finding the new term rather hard to define, "they're going to serenade the newly married couple, the bride and groom, and sing and make a lot of noise and things until they come out on the porch and show themselves and then they have to set up a treat for the crowd, cigars and things. Mike Bullen and his gang have got a big dry-goods box made into a horse-fiddle with a lot of rosin on it, and it screeches something terrible, and Dick Bates has swiped his father's cornet, and Tom and me was going to see it all."

" But," objected the truthful Eddie, " you told father you were going over to Fatty Bullen's? "

" We were," said Tom.

" Yes," added Richard, " we was going there first and then going to meet the gang."

" I'm going anyhow," announced Tom with sudden determination.

" If you go, I'll go too," asserted Richard.

" But what'll Dad say? " questioned Eddie, shocked at their daring.

" He can't do any worse than lick us," said Tom, " and it's going to be worth a licking."

" He might come after us and make us march home," suggested Richard.

" How's he going to find out where we have gone? "

" Eddie'll tell him."

Tom turned and regarded his youngest brother with a threatening manner. He felt that, as Richard had suggested, here lay a possibility of betrayal. While Eddie might wish to keep their secret, he had the habit of telling the truth. If Dad asked him where his brothers had gone, what could he say? Something of the same course of thought was going through Eddie's mind. He foresaw himself in a painful dilemma. Either he would have to betray Tom and Richard, or else he would have to fib to Dad. He did not wish to do either. Suddenly a way out of the difficulty dawned on him, a solution not without its personal advantages.

" I won't tell," he said, " for I'm going with you."

" Naw, you can't. You're too —" Richard began, but Tom hushed him up quickly.

" Sure, Eddie can come along if he wants to," he directed. " He'll enjoy all the fun as much as we will."

" All right," said Richard, " you can come if you want to."

Eddie could hardly believe it possible that they were going to permit his company. Ordinarily, when any exciting adventure was in prospect, they ran off and left him. And he did so much want to see what a charivari was like. In the excitement of departure he almost forgot that he was being disobedient. With his two brothers he slipped out of the yard, carefully avoiding the front gate, and soon the three of them formed a joyful and excited part of the throng that had already congregated about the Sweeney cottage. They watched with eagerness the dry-goods box brought up that was to constitute the horse-fiddle. They participated loudly in the repeated calls of " Come on out," " Bring out the bride." They applauded vociferously as an impromptu choir bawled out, " Oh, my darling Nellie Gray," and such other favorites.

They were excitedly enjoying it all, skipping hither and thither through the crowd to watch and discuss each new development. They had forgotten that they were disobedient fugitives. Suddenly the rude hand of an unkind fate descended. It seized Tom and Richard firmly by the collar.

" You boys come right home," said their father's voice in tones so stern that they hardly recognized it.

Painfully conscious of the unwelcome notice of the multitude, burning with shame at the jeers and catcalls from the other boys that reached their ears, anxiously wondering what further punishment still awaited them, the two boys in their father's grasp, with Eddie, frightened almost to sobbing, trailing in the rear, marched silently homeward. At their own door Mr. Randall released them.

"Go right up-stairs and go to bed," he said sternly. "In the morning I will punish you for your disobedience."

With their zest for adventure turned to bitter shame, with no words among themselves, for one evening without their mother's kiss, the three of them crept silently into bed wondering what new disgrace and terror the morrow would bring. Meanwhile their parents downstairs debated a fit punishment.

"All three of them deserve a sound thrashing," asserted Mr. Randall. "I forbade their going over to Bullens' because I had heard about the charivari that was planned for tonight, and such affairs are no place for youngsters."

"But Eddie," protested Mrs. Randall, "you wouldn't whip Eddie."

" They all three disobeyed. All three must
be punished."

" Eddie must not be whipped," said his
mother firmly. " I don't think he's as much
to blame as the others. They are older and
ought to know better."

" Well," said her husband, " I won't whip
any of them. I'll punish them all alike.
They must *learn* once and for all that they
must do as they are told."

So it was decided, and it was three fearful
youngsters who came down to breakfast the
next morning — came down late, in the vain
hope that Dad might be gone already to the
office, came down together, feeling that there
is strength even in the unity of conscious guilt.

Their hope was disappointed. Dad was still
there, though he had long ago finished his
breakfast. Plainly, he had been waiting for
them. They paused at the door of the dining-
room and anxiously studied his face. How
were they to be punished? Was it to be a
licking? Would he whip them all — Eddie,
too? — they wondered.

" You three boys disobeyed me last night,"
said Mr. Randall without preliminaries. " I
forbade any of you going out of the yard.

You all three went. You told me you were
going to Bullens'. You went to that disgraceful charivari at Sweeneys'. As a punishment
you are not to go outside of your own yard for
one week from today."

"Not even to school?" asked Tom, hardly
believing his ears. This was a new, protracted
sort of penalty little to his liking.

"Not even to school," said Mr. Randall.

"Oh, goody!" cried Richard.

"But, Dad," protested Eddie, blank dismay
written in his countenance, "I'll lose my perfect attendance record."

"That can not be helped," said Mr. Randall inexorably. "You should have thought
of the possible penalties for disobedience before you went away last night."

They were three stunned youngsters whom
he left behind him when he went to his office.
Even their customary breakfast appetites
failed them. The more they thought about
their punishment the more severe and unendurable it seemed.

"I'd rather have taken a couple of lickings
and had them over with," complained Richard.
"This lasts a whole week."

"And that isn't the worst of it," groaned

Tom. "Just wait till the fellows find it out."

"Oh, gee, that's fierce!" exclaimed Richard, "I never thought of that!"

Bitterly as they had felt the shame of capture the evening before, its memories now faded before the terrifying prospect of what would occur when the other boys learned of their incarceration for a week. Already they foresaw a week of unendurable captivity while a jeering crowd of boys and girls gathered each day after school outside their fence to taunt them.

The whistled call of Fatty Bullen en route to school elicited no response. Shamefacedly Tom and Richard folded their napkins and left the table, creeping off to the barn to stay safely out of sight till the last of the boys was in the schoolroom. Eddie lingered at the table, waiting till his mother had come into the room, and trying then to find comfort in her presence, but it seemed somehow as if overnight a great wall had sprung up between them. He waited in vain for her to begin the conversation.

"Don't you think," he said at last, "that Miss McGuffey will wonder where I am."

"I don't think so. Your father was going

to leave a note for the principal explaining your absence."

"Oh!" exclaimed Eddie. He had had some vague hope that his absence might be accounted for by illness. He resented having his punishment reported to the principal, to the teacher, to everybody and anybody. To be punished this way was bad enough without having it talked about. A wave of anger and resentment against his father crept into his heart.

The sad look on the face of her youngest was too much for the mother heart. Mrs. Randall knew how proud Eddie had been of his perfect attendance record. She felt she must try to do something for her small son.

"Eddie, dear," she suggested, "perhaps when your father comes home to luncheon, if you go up to him and say you are sorry and promise that you will obey him hereafter he may let you go to school again this afternoon."

"But," said Eddie, "I'm not sorry."

With that he stalked defiantly from the room to join his brothers, leaving a mother thoroughly amazed and perplexed by his surprising conduct. She could not imagine what baleful influence had suddenly turned her sweet-tempered, gentle child into a desperate, defiant youth.

Yet Eddie down in his heart was sorry. Right gladly he would have gone to his father as mother had suggested, if there had been only himself to consider. The anger and resentment he had felt against his father had lasted hardly until he reached the porch. It was all he could do to keep the tears back and to keep his voice from quivering as he had announced that he was not sorry. Oh, he *was* sorry, so sorry it had all happened. But there were his brothers. They had trusted him. They had let him go with them. They had decided that he was " game." He must stand by them now. So long as they endured their punishment, so must he. He wished he could explain to his mother how he felt about it. Perhaps, though, she wouldn't understand. There were some things women didn't understand.

As the time for the noon recess approached, all three of them sought refuge in the house, apparently unmindful of the troop of boys who went by whistling and calling for them. They ate their midday meal for once in silence, attempting no part in the conversation, while Mr. and Mrs. Randall chatted pleasantly to-

gether, paying no attention to them beyond
seeing that their plates were filled. After the
dreary meal was over and Mr. Randall had
gone again to the office, they sat uneasily about
the dining-room until the last school-bell gave
them warning that it was safe for them to ad-
journ to the yard.

Tom and Richard headed for the barn in
search of pastime, but Eddie seated himself
on the back porch to think it over. Surely
there must be some way out of it. To go on
living like this for six more days seemed unbearable. If only he could talk it all over with
old Jonas. A suddenly formed resolve seized
him. He went into the living-room to find
his mother. "If I give my parole, like prison-
ers do in war, to go away and come back in
an hour," he asked, "may I leave the yard?
I promise not to go anywhere you wouldn't
want me to."

Mrs. Randall gravely debated the question.
She wondered if Eddie had changed his mind
and wanted to go to his father's office to say
he was sorry. She forbore to ask. Perhaps
he wanted to go to see that queer old man
whose remarks he was always quoting. She
decided to give her permission. "If you will

give your word of honor to return in one hour you may go."

As fast as his lame leg would carry him, Eddie went hurrying down the street to old Jonas's, and soon was pouring out the whole story to the one-legged veteran, who listened sympathetically as always.

"And Tom says," Eddie concluded, "that Dad's only doing it to be mean because we quit kissing him good night."

"No, sir," old Jonas answered, vigorously shaking his beard in disapproval, "it's nothing like that. Your Dad was perfectly right. 'Shivarees' are no place for young boys. Sometimes the crowd gets to drinking and gets pretty rough. Once when I was a youngster an old man got mad at the noise and fired a load of buckshot into the crowd and some was pretty bad hurt. Besides, Eddie, whether it was right or wrong for you to go, it was against orders. In every house the father is the general, or he ought to be, and you boys are the soldiers. It's the business of good soldiers to do what they are told without asking questions. A fine army it would be if everybody did as they liked. And who's got a better right to give you orders than your father? As long

as you boys are living in your father's house
and eating his food and wearing the clothes
he buys for you, it's up to you all to do what
he tells you. No, sir, you boys are rebels.
You've been licked just like we licked the
Rebels at Gettysburg and all them places.
The best thing for you boys to do is to holler
for peace with honor and to holler quick."

"How'll we go about it?" Eddie asked.
Since old Jonas had explained it, he saw now
how much in the wrong he and his brothers
had been.

"Why don't you approach your dad with a
flag of truce?" suggested Jonas.

"Gee," said Eddie, his military spirit kindling at the thought, "that would be great,
wouldn't it?"

So that night, shortly after Mr. Randall returned home, the three boys filed into the room
where he was sitting. Eddie led the way
carrying a white handkerchief pinned to a cane.
Their father looked up wonderingly as they
approached.

"What's this," he asked, " a flag of truce?"

"That's what," said Eddie delightedly, giving way to Tom as spokesman.

" We wish to say, sir," said Tom, " that we surrender. We are sorry we disobeyed you last night, and if you will let us go to school tomorrow, we will try hereafter to do what we are told."

" On that condition," Mr. Randall replied, " the sentence is suspended and your parole is accepted. You need no longer stay in the yard."

" Oh, Dad," cried Eddie, joyfully, dropping his flag and rushing forward for a kiss, " it's a peace with honor, isn't it? "

" But only Eddie kissed you," said Mrs. Randall disappointedly that night after the three were safe in bed. " I hoped that Tom and Richard would, too."

" They'd have liked to," Mr. Randall answered, " and they knew I knew they'd have liked to, so let's let it go at that. We men understand one another."

CHAPTER FIVE

"I'M giving it for Mr. Wilson's nephew and niece who are visiting us," explained Mrs. Wilson.

"How lovely!" exclaimed Mrs. Randall.

"I'm asking only about twenty of the boys and girls — only the nicest ones."

"Of course," said Mrs. Randall with understanding.

"I'm sending invitations to two of your boys, Tom and Richard. I purposely did not invite Eddie. I felt sure you would not want him to go."

"No," said Eddie's mother, rather doubtfully, "I suppose it would be better if he stayed home."

"You see," her guest went on, "he is so much younger than the others, and then, on account of his lameness, I felt that you would not wish him to be going out at night."

"No, of course not," said Mrs. Randall absently. To tell the truth her mother heart was worrying not a little as to how her youngest would take it when he learned that his brothers had been invited to a party and that he had been omitted. Eddie did not like being left out of things, or being made to feel that he was different from other boys. It was quite true that his mother did not relish the idea of his going anywhere at night. She always worried about him whenever he was out of her sight. There was always the fear that he might fall and hurt his poor, lame leg, or of some mishap to the iron brace he had to wear. If anything happened to it, Eddie would be helpless. Probably it was just as well that he was not to be invited, though she knew he would be much disappointed. But she was wondering what she could plan to offset Eddie's disappointment. She and his father must give up the whole evening to him and arrange something he would like. So busy was she with her own thoughts that she hardly listened to the rest of Mrs. Wilson's conversation.

At noon the next day the invitations arrived. Black Maggie brought them in while the boys were at the table, two of them, in square, white envelopes addressed to " Master Thomas Ran-

dall, Jr.," and " Master Richard P. Randall."
With a feeling of vast importance at receiving
mail addressed to themselves, the two boys
hastened to open the envelopes. Tom read his
aloud:

> Mr. and Mrs. Henry R. Wilson request the pleas-
> ure of the company of Master Thomas Randall,
> Junior, on Friday evening, the twenty-fifth, at eight
> o'clock, to meet their nephew and niece, Master
> William and Miss Edna Wilson.
> If convenient you will please call for Miss Ida
> Jones.

Dick's invitation was similarly worded except that he was asked to call for Carrie Wallace.

" Oh, great! " cried Tom, " it's a party.
See my invitation, Dad."

" See mine, too," chimed in Richard.

As Mr. Randall duly admired both invitations, his wife was anxiously watching the face
of her youngest to see how he took it. At first
she noted nothing but boyish curiosity. Eddie was pleased and interested in the unusual
sight of his brothers getting letters of their
very own. Then, as Tom read his invitation
aloud and Richard followed suit, an expression of incredulous dismay came into Eddie's

face. Where was his invitation? At first he could not believe it possible that he was not to be asked. Yet that must be it. If they had wanted him, his invitation would have come with the others. No, he was not to get any. They did not want him at the party. Nobody wanted him. He was a cripple. People didn't want cripples at parties. The expression of dismay in his face gave way to one of bitterness, bitterness toward all the world.

Just then his father unthinkingly asked: " Where's yours, Eddie? Didn't you get one, too? "

Too late Mrs. Randall shot a glance of warning at her husband, but the damage was done. Eddie gulped. In spite of his efforts to restrain them, two great tears rolled down his cheeks. His voice quivered dolefully as he answered:

" I didn't get any. I guess they don't want me there."

" Never mind," said his father with affected cheerfulness, " you're too young to be going to parties."

" And too lame," Eddie burst out, rising hastily from the table and hobbling from the room. He just hated to have any one see him cry, but the tears would not be kept back.

"Gee," said Tom, "it's too bad they didn't ask the kid."

"Sure it is," added Richard, "and I'll bet they're going to have ice-cream, too; loads of it."

Mrs. Randall half rose from her chair to follow Eddie from the room, but changed her mind. What was there she could say to him? She must talk it over with her husband. As Tom and Richard dashed out in haste to show their invitations to the rest of the boys, she asked anxiously: "Don't you think I had better ask Mrs. Wilson if she won't invite Eddie? The poor little fellow is so disappointed."

"Don't you do anything of the sort," Mr. Randall advised. "You pamper that child far too much. He must learn that he can not have everything he wants. It is just as well that he isn't going."

"But he hasn't much fun," the mother protested. "There are so many of the games the boys play that he can't take part in. I wish he could go."

"Well, he isn't asked, so that settles it," said Mr. Randall as he went off to business.

But he was mistaken; it did not settle it. Mrs. Randall and Mrs. Wilson met that afternoon in Kendall's grocery. Eddie's mother regarded their meeting as almost providential. As they chatted, she was making up her mind to tell Mrs. Wilson how disappointed her small son had been and to urge that he, too, be asked.

Mrs. Wilson, however, saved her the trouble. " Oh, my dear," she said, " there's something I almost forgot to tell you. I changed my mind and asked Eddie after all. You see, I had forgotten to include in my list that nice little Floribel Finch who lives next door to you. I sent her an invitation today. I wanted to have the same number of boys and girls and I couldn't think of another boy to invite, so I addressed an invitation to Eddie and mailed it today. You don't really mind, do you? "

" No, indeed I don't," said Mrs. Randall heartily. " I'm really delighted that you asked him. He was so disappointed."

She hurried home with the good news, hoping to find Eddie there, for it was time for school to be out, but already he had hurried away to old Jonas Tucker's tobacco shop and was telling his troubles to the one-legged veteran in whom he always found a sympathetic and understanding listener.

"Don't you care, Eddie," said old Jonas consolingly, "maybe you wouldn't have a good time at the party if you did get to go."

"But people always have a good time at parties," protested Eddie. "That's what they have parties for."

"It ain't where you are or what you are doing that makes a good time. A good time is here," said old Jonas, pointing to his head. "It is what you think that makes good times and bad times."

"I don't quite understand," said Eddie soberly. Thinking you were having a good time staying away from a party was beyond his philosophy.

"Now, if I was so minded," old Jonas went on, "I could sit out here in front of my shop having a bad time. I might be growling because I can't get around much to see things. I might get mad every time a man came walking by here on two legs at thinking I had only one. But, Eddie, that ain't my way. I have a good time just sitting here, and reading my paper, and watching people pass, and feeling thankful that my little friend, Eddie Randall, has two legs —"

" A leg and a half," interrupted Eddie. It was a standing joke between them. And old Jonas was the only person in the whole world with whom Eddie could joke about his lameness. He never felt badly when Jonas talked about it.

" A leg and a half," amended Jonas, " to get here afternoons to see me."

" But when you were young, as young as me," protested Eddie, still unconvinced, " didn't you like to go to parties? "

" I suppose I did," the old man answered, " but I can't remember enjoying any of them as much as I thought I would beforehand. You see, Eddie, it ain't all gold that glitters. There's lots of things we see shining ahead of us that looks mighty fine, but when we get up close they ain't worth having. It's like the pyrites that fool so many gold-hunters—fool's gold they call it. You mustn't let the glitter of things deceive you. If you don't get to go to the party, and stay home with your dad and mother, I'll wager you'll have a better time than if you went. Remember the time they wouldn't let you go fishing, and the airship came down, and you saw it, and Tom and Richard didn't."

"Yes, but this time is different," Eddie objected. "A party's real gold."

"I'll admit it glitters, but lots of things glitter," was Jonas's parting shot. "Be sure and tell me about it afterward."

"Sure I will," said Eddie.

Despite old Jonas's attempted consolation, Eddie, when he reached home, was still as despondent as ever. With shining eyes his mother watched him as he took his seat at the table. The invitation had come and lay hidden under his napkin. He took his seat looking sullen and ugly, and then: "Oh, Mother, oh, Dad, look!" he shrieked in an ecstasy of joy. "I'm invited, too."

"How nice," exclaimed his mother, as if it were an entire surprise to her.

"Of course," said Mr. Randall, casting a searching glance at his wife to see if she had brought it about.

Eddie's hands trembled so in his excitement and joy that he could hardly open the envelop. He read the contents to himself, blushing vividly at the last line.

" Who are you to take? " questioned Tom curiously.

" Whom," corrected his mother.

" Eddie's got a girl, Eddie's got a girl," Richard began tauntingly, but a sharp glance from his father quickly silenced him.

" She's asked me to call for Floribel Finch," stammered Eddie, blushing again as he mentioned the name of his divinity.

Ever since Floribel had moved into the house next door, he had worshiped her, though from afar. He was sure she was the very prettiest little girl he had ever seen. Though they were in the same room at school, and she had been in attendance now for several weeks, he had exchanged hardly a dozen words with her. To escort her to a party was far beyond any heights his ambition had reached. He thus far had never even dared to walk home from school with her and carry her books, as some of the other boys did. And now, oh joy, he was to take her to the party!

Suddenly a new fear smote him. How was he ever to muster up courage to ask her to go with him? It was a momentous problem. He wondered how his brothers had gone about inviting the girls they were to take. " You're

going to take Ida Jones, aren't you?" he asked
Tom, trying hard to seem disinterested, yet
with a new warmth in his heart from a sense of
comradeship.

"Yep," replied Tom carelessly, "I told her
about it this afternoon."

"And I'm going to take Carrie Wallace,"
chimed in Dick. "I didn't have to ask her.
She asked me this afternoon what time I was
coming for her."

There was not much enlightenment for
Eddie in either of his brother's answers. Had
he only known the truth, they, too, had suf-
fered from the pangs of bashfulness and had
been as puzzled as he as to the best method of
procedure. They, too, had arrived at the same
conclusion that Eddie now reached and had
privately sought their mother's advice. Eddie
waited until his brothers had gone out into the
yard to play, and his father had left the room.

"Mother," he said, "how am I going to ask
Floribel?"

"You see her every day at school," his
mother suggested; "why don't you ask her
there?"

"I don't want to do that," he faltered.
"The fellows might tease me about it."

" Why not write her a note, and I will mail it for you tonight? "

" What'll I say? "

" Get a pen and ink, and I'll help you with it."

So Eddie, at his mother's dictation, wrote:

Dear Floribel:
May I call for you about half-past seven on Friday evening and take you to the party at Mrs. Wilson's?

" How'll I sign it? " he questioned, as he laboriously finished the note, after rejecting three sheets because he felt that the writing was not up to his usual standard.

"Anyway you like," his mother called out as she was summoned to the kitchen for a consultation with Maggie.

After a few minutes of painful deliberation, Eddie wrote, " Your true little friend," and sealed it up without waiting to show it to his mother.

For the next four days, until the night of the party, Eddie lived in a whirl of excitement. For two whole days he did not go near old Jonas. He just hung around the house, waiting eagerly for an answer to his note. What if she had not received it? What if she replied that she was not going, or that she had another escort? Though each day he saw Floribel at school, they exchanged no conversation on the subject. From her self-conscious air, whenever he was in the vicinity, he was almost certain she must have received his note, yet he did not dare to ask. At last, two days before the party, her answer came. Eddie was thankful that his brothers had finished their breakfasts and disappeared before the postman arrived. Only he and his mother were at the table when he received the note, which read:

Miss Floribel Finch accepts with Plesure Master Eddie Randall's Invitashun for Friday evening.

Somehow Eddie felt vaguely disappointed in the missive's impersonality. He had hoped that his statement that he was her true little friend would bring a similarly responsive answer.

"Is Floribel going with you?" his mother asked.

"Yes'm," he answered, but he did not offer to show her Floribel's note. He felt that it was too precious even for mother's eyes to see. Whenever he was off by himself all through that day and the next, he took the note from his pocket and read and reread it. In the schoolroom, too, more often than usual, he found his eyes turning toward Floribel's golden curls. She was no longer just the girl next door; she was the goddess who had condescended to go to the party with him.

And for once he kept a secret from old Jonas. Though he told his comrade that he had been invited to the party and that he was going, he said never a word about taking Floribel, for thus does love intrude itself rudely between the understanding and friendship of men.

When Friday night came — and never a night so long in coming — promptly at half-past seven Eddie presented himself at the Finches' front door and rang the bell, his heart palpitating wildly.

"Come in and sit down," said Mr. Finch. "Floribel will be down in a moment."

Eddie seated himself on the edge of the sofa; Mr. Finch went on reading his paper, paying no attention to him. Eddie tried to think of something to say for politeness' sake but failed. So he just sat there fidgeting nervously.

By and by down came Floribel escorted by her mother, her golden curls freshly done, her

starched white skirts standing out stiffly from
her white stockings, a wonderful blue cape covering her shoulders, and a great bow of ribbon
of the same hue adorning her hair, to Eddie's
eyes the most wonderful vision he had ever
seen.

Mindful of his manners, he got up as they
entered the room, and stood there far too embarrassed for words.

"My, how nice you both look," said Mrs.
Finch. "Now run along, children, so you
won't be late."

With the width of the sidewalk between
them, the two marched up the street, both too
painfully self-conscious to attempt conversation. Not a word did either of them utter till
they reached the corner of Wood Street.

"Let's take the railroad-track," said Floribel, "it's shorter."

"Yes," said Eddie, "it's shorter."

He would much have preferred going around
the other way. It was hard work for him to
walk on the railroad-ties. He took a long step
with one leg and a short one with the other.
He had to watch his feet constantly to keep
from stumbling. But the spirit of gallantry
was his. If Floribel had wanted to walk up

the creek, he would have gone.   Together they
started up the tracks.

" Isn't the moon pretty tonight?" said Floribel.

Up till that moment Eddie had forgotten
there was a moon.   He gazed upward, his lame
foot caught on a tie, he stumbled, tried vainly
to regain his balance, and crashed full length
on the ties.

Floribel stood aghast at her courtier's mishap.   His hands all soiled and bruised, Eddie,
overcome with confusion, scrambled to his feet.
Though he had twisted his lame leg painfully,
he set his teeth and said nothing about it.

" Oh," shrilled Floribel, " you've torn your
pants!"

Sure enough, right across the knee of his best
trousers was a great gaping tear.   His stock-
ing under it, too, was torn and the bare flesh
showed through.   The pain of his aching limb
was forgotten in the tragedy of this new catas-
trophe.

What should he do about it?   He was
tempted to leave Floribel right where she stood
and to go home as fast as he could.   How was
it possible for him to go to the party with that
great gaping tear?   Every one would look at

it, and the boys would laugh—yes, and the
girls, too.   Yet he felt he must go on.   He
could not leave Floribel there alone.

"Come on," he said almost gruffly.

"You're sure you didn't hurt yourself when
you fell?" asked Floribel.   Her first feeling
had been one of vexation at her cavalier for his
awkwardness, but that quickly passed.   Naturally a kind-hearted little girl, she really was
concerned about his mishap, and, besides, she
had made up her mind weeks ago that she
liked Eddie Randall very much, his standing in the schoolroom compelling her admiration.

"Naw, I'm not hurt.   That's nothing.   I
often fall," protested Eddie, determined to put
on as brave a front as possible before his lady-
love.

Timidly Floribel's hand reached out and
seized his and silently they trudged down the
tracks together.   In the new joy of feeling
her fingers clasped in his, Eddie for the moment forgot his woes, almost forgot that his
pants — his best pants — were torn.   He was
having his first experience with that eternal
sympathy of woman — the needed hand
reached out so silently, so tenderly, and oh, so

often, to help us menfolk over the rough, cruel places in life's path.   The very touch of Floribel's fingers brought sweet comfort to him and filled him with an unwonted sense of peace and happiness.

No further word was spoken between them until they turned in at the Wilsons' gate.   As the lights of the house, all prepared for the party, loomed up before them, the vexatious problem in Floribel's mind found voice.

" What are you going to do about your pants? " she questioned timidly.

" Pooh!   I don't mind a little thing like that," replied Eddie, made valorous by the sympathetic touch of her soft fingers.

But he did mind — very much.   It was one thing to say courageous things out there in the dark.   It was quite another thing to face a merry crowd all in their best in the brilliantly lighted rooms — to face them with a ragged tear clear across the knee of his trousers.   Fortunately in the bustle of arriving guests no one noticed his plight.   He hung his cap on the hat-rack and slunk into the living-room where he hastened to find a seat on the sofa.   He discovered after some experimenting that if he sat with one knee crossed over the other, no one could see the tear. So there he sat in a stiff, uncomfortable attitude.

Floribel, too, found that in the midst of the merry throng things took on a different aspect. Though she felt sorry for Eddie, she did not feel brave enough to stick by his side. She was afraid everybody would laugh at his torn trousers. She went up-stairs to lay off her cloak and when she came down sought a corner of the room as far distant as possible from Eddie. Though occasionally she cast a shy glance in his direction, she kept carefully away from him all the evening. She could not endure the thought of hearing her own particular cavalier jeered at.

Meanwhile, Eddie just sat there, carefully keeping his legs crossed.

"Come on, Eddie," said Mrs. Wilson, "we're going to play post-office. Don't you want to play?"

"No'm," said Eddie. "I'd rather sit here."

So all the long evening Eddie sat there on the sofa all by himself. His legs grew stiff and painful, but he did not dare move them. One foot went to sleep, and he was in an agony of discomfort, but more than anything he dreaded discovery of his mishap: so, somehow, he managed to endure it. The other guests, with all the thoughtlessness of youth, paid little attention to him, being intent on their own pleasures.

About ten o'clock Mrs. Wilson threw open the doors into the dining-room.

"Come on, boys and girls," she said; "it's time for refreshments. Get your partners."

Eddie sat there aghast at the announcement. After all his pains to conceal his plight, discovery now seemed inevitable. He felt he just could not get up now and go out to the dining-room with the others. But what about Floribel? He had brought her there. He would be expected to take her out for refreshments. As he looked about for her, he saw her merrily flitting into the dining-room with another couple. She had not even waited for him. Well, now, certainly he would not go into the dining-room.

Mrs. Wilson, busy with serving her guests, did not note his absence from the room. As he sat there he could hear the shouts and laughter that came as the mottoes were pulled apart and the paper caps donned. A great lump rose in his throat. Parties were no fun. He wished he had not come. Old Jonas had been right

about it.   He would have had a much better
time if he had stayed at home.   He took advantage of the absence of every one from the
room to stretch his legs, hastily crossing them
again every time he thought he heard any one
coming.

He heard the clatter of spoons as the ice-
cream was passed.   Ice-cream — and he was
not getting any of it!   He decided to slip
quietly out and go home.   He rose to his feet
and then sat down again.   No, he didn't dare
to try that.   Some one would be sure to hear
him, and he would be discovered.   And there
was Floribel, too.   He must wait and take her
home.   So he sat there, alone, wretched, miserable, a pathetic little figure on the great sofa.

By and by the other children came trooping
back.   No one seemed to have missed him and
he felt sadly glad of it.   Mrs. Wilson spied
him still sitting on the sofa and could not recall
having served him with any supper.

"Why, Eddie Randall," she said, "I don't
believe you had any ice-cream."

"I didn't want any," he said solemnly, his
words almost choking him.   If she said another word to him, he felt that he was going to
cry and be disgraced forever,

Something in his face warned Mrs. Wilson of his state of mind, and she forbore to question him further. Anyhow, she remembered, the ice-cream was all gone. It was Eddie's own fault if he had had none. Besides, she must see to the dancing.

As eleven o'clock came, the girls began slipping out of the room in groups of two and three to get their coats up-stairs, the boys following a little later as far as the hall. Eddie waited till the last and followed a group of boys out. He felt safer now. Probably in the dimmer light of the hall no one would notice his pants. By the time he got his cap and reached the foot of the staircase at least half of the couples had said their adieux and departed. One by one the girls came down and joined their escorts. Last in line, he stood there waiting for Floribel. Finally every one had gone but him. Mrs. Wilson and her niece came down the stairs together.

"Waiting to say good night?" Mrs. Wilson called out, as she spied the solitary little figure at the foot of the stairs.

"No'm," said Eddie truthfully, rather than politely, "I'm waiting for Floribel."

"Why, she left long ago," said Mrs. Wilson's niece. " She went home with your brother Tom and Carrie Wallace."

In a daze of despair Eddie left the Wilson house. Miserable, despondent, bitter toward all the world, he trudged home alone along the railroad tracks. Why, oh, why had he ever gone to the party? Old Jonas was right. Parties weren't gold. He had not had any fun at all. He had not even had any of the ice-cream. And Floribel— probably Floribel would never speak to him again, would never want to see him ever again. He had disgraced her and himself forever.

As he entered the house just behind his brothers, it was with great relief he heard Dad say: " You boys hustle right upstairs to bed. You've stayed up late enough as it is. We'll talk about the party tomorrow."

He was glad there were no explanations to make that evening. He was glad that even mother, as she kissed him good night, seemed to take it for granted that he had had a good time. It was all too terrible, too distressing to talk about to any one.

At breakfast the next morning he let his brothers do all the talking. In the afternoon, as usual, he went to see old Jonas.

" And how was the party? " old Jonas asked. " You remember you promised to tell me all about it."

" There's nothing to tell," said Eddie.

CHAPTER SIX

ACCORDING TO CODE

"I GOT ten demerits in school today," announced Edward Haverford Randall.

"What for?" asked old Jonas Tucker. "Were you a bad boy?"

"I don't know," answered Eddie thoughtfully.

For a moment or two the grizzled veteran meditatively studied the face of ten and then commanded: "Tell me about it. When a fellow don't know whether he's been bad or not, there's sure something behind it."

"It was this way," began Eddie. "Fatty Bullen threw a paper-wad at Froggie Sweeney, and Froggie ducked, and it hit the blackboard and stuck there, and teacher saw it."

"So," chuckled old Jonas, "they still throw paper-wads, do they? They did that when I was a lad."

"Yes," replied Eddie, "some of the boys still do it. So the teacher asked who did it, and

nobody said a word. Then she asked me,
' Eddie, do you know who threw that paper-
wad?' I said I did. Then she asked, ' Who
was it?'"

"You didn't tell, did you?" queried Jonas,
assuming a horrified air.

"No," replied Eddie, "I didn't. I was going to, and then I remembered."

"Remembered what?"

"What Brother Tom said."

"What was that?"

"Tom says no fellow that's game ever
tattles."

"Tom's right," old Jonas affirmed approvingly. "What happened then?"

"She said she would give me ten demerits
unless I told her, and I wouldn't tell."

"So she didn't find out, did she?"

"Oh, yes, she did," said Eddie. "Mary Et-
tinger told her."

"Girls most always do," commented Jonas,
nodding understandingly.

"But you don't think I was bad for not telling?" questioned Eddie anxiously.

"Yes and no," replied the old man thoughtfully. "You see, Eddie, there's two sides to
every question. From the teacher's point of

view I suppose you undoubtedly was bad. It's her business to keep order in the school, and to find out as best she can who's to blame for the mischief. Looking at it another way — the man's way of seeing it — I think you did exactly right."

"And you don't think I ought to have got the demerits?"

"I didn't say that either," old Jonas objected. "She told you to do something, you decided not to do it; it was up to you to take whatever punishment was coming. A man — a real man — can't ever be a tattle-tale. If he's done something himself, and is asked about it, why, of course, it's right for him to tell. There's only himself to be blamed and punished for it. If it's something another fellow did, he has got to keep his mouth shut, no matter what it costs. That's according to code."

"According to code?" Eddie repeated with a puzzled air. "What's code mean?"

"A code is something everybody has agreed to. For instance, people get together and say this is right and that's wrong, and that's the code of law. Mostly law-codes are written down and passed by legislatures and such. But all codes are not written. It is the code of the sea for a captain to be the last to leave his sinking ship; it's railroad-code for the engineer to stick to his engine even when he sees a collision coming; it's the code of men to save women and children first when there's a fire."

" I think I understand now," said Eddie.

" So a long time ago, centuries, maybe, men decided that one man mustn't tell on another man. I don't know as it is written down anywhere, but that has been man's code ever since."

" Isn't it women's code, too? "

" I can't say as to that. You see, Eddie, I never had a wife nor a daughter, so I don't know much about womenfolks. Maybe the women never agreed to it, and maybe that's why girls tell teacher more often than boys do. Maybe women have a code of their own. There are lots of ways they are different and better than men. Women, though, often don't see things the way men do. Very likely your teacher is sure she was right and that you were wrong, but, just the same, I say you hadn't ought to have told."

" I wonder what mother will say about it," said Eddie soberly, more to himself than to old Jonas.

"Mothers, women that have sons of their own," declared the old man, "are pretty apt to understand the code.   I'll bet your mother will say you did perfectly right."

"I hope she does," said Eddie doubtfully; "it's the very first time I ever had any demerits."

He had contemplated putting off telling his mother about it until his weekly report came home, but somehow it was hard to keep secrets from mother. He found himself telling her all about it that night as she massaged his leg after he was in bed.

"Miss McGuffey had no business trying to make you tattle," exclaimed his mother indignantly. "You did perfectly right not to tell."

"I knew you would understand," cried Eddie gleefully.

"I'm going right along with you to school in the morning and give that teacher a piece of my mind."

"Oh, mother," cried Eddie in alarm, "please don't do anything like that!"

"Why not?" asked Mrs. Randall, puzzled at his perturbation.

"'Cause," he explained falteringly, "the fel-

lows all guy a fellow whose mother comes to
school."

" Well," she persisted, " at least I'm going to
write her a note."

" Oh, no, mother," he begged, " please don't
do that either."

" Why not?   It certainly was not fair to give
you all those demerits?"

" Oh, that's all right," her son explained.
" If I don't do what she tells me to, it's up to
me to take the consequences.   That's according to code."

" What funny notions you do get," said his
mother as she kissed him good night.   " I'll
talk with your father about it."

A good deal to Mrs. Randall's amazement,
her husband was quite in accord with Eddie.
She could not understand it.   She knew that
he as well as she had been proud of Eddie's
long record of perfect behavior.

" Don't you interfere," cautioned her husband.   " The boy has got to learn to fight his
own battles.   You would make a mollycoddle
of him if you had your way.   I'm glad to see
that he is getting spunk enough to defy the
teacher once in a while.   Don't you do anything about it."

"Well, maybe you know best," said Mrs. Randall, still unconvinced.

So nothing more was done about it, and no comments were made on Eddie's report-card when it came home. Despite the disgrace of ten demerits, life at school and at home went on as usual. Yet there was one difference, observable only to Eddie himself. With a little pang of regret, he noted that Miss McGuffey did not seem to trust him quite as much as before. Although he got just as good marks as formerly, and she always spoke as pleasantly to him as before, he could not help noticing that now when she wanted some little errand done, she asked some one else to do it — generally one of the girls. Then two weeks later came Eddie's disgrace.

The morning was rainy. Eddie, starting from home a little earlier than usual because the pavements were slippery, arrived at the school building twenty minutes before nine. At the door he met Fatty Bullen and Froggie Sweeney, driven to cover by the rain. As it was Friday morning, when special exercises were held in the assembly-room, they went directly there instead of to their classroom, being the first arrivals.

" Oh, gee! " cried Froggie exultantly as they entered, " look what's doin'! "

With amazed eyes the three of them gazed at the rostrum. Along one side of the room had stood a great case of stuffed birds, presented to the school by one of the trustees. During the night some one had gotten into the building and had broken open this case. There on the rostrum in each teacher's place was a bird. On Principal Phillips's desk was a great ruffed owl. At the piano, where Miss Estep, always clad in somber black, played for the singing, was a great black crow. Miss McGuffey's chair was occupied by a lopsided crane that grotesquely reminded the boys of her long, thin neck. Each bird, in fact, had been carefully placed to caricature the teacher whose place it occupied.

" Ain't it great! " cried Fatty Bullen admiringly.

" I wonder who did it," said Eddie.

" We're the first here," declared Froggie with the wisdom of past performances. " Old Phillips will be sure to blame it on us."

" But we didn't do it," protested Eddie, adding as an afterthought, " at least, I didn't have anything to do with it."

"Me neither," said Fatty.

"Nor me," echoed Froggie; "but all the same he'll make us try to tell who did."

"Tell you what," suggested Fatty with sudden inspiration, "let's agree not to answer any questions. Let him find out as best he can. If everybody'll do that, how's he going to find out anything?"

"Great!" cried Froggie. "Whatever he asks, we'll just up and say, 'We decline to answer any questions.'"

"That's the ticket," said Fatty. "How about it, Limpy?"

Eddie was cogitating. Mother and old Jonas and brother Tom were all agreed that a boy must not be a tattle-tale. If he had known who took out the birds, he felt that it would be according to code not to tell. So long as he knew nothing whatever about it, what harm could there be in refusing to answer any questions?

"All right," he said, "I agree."

"Cross your heart and hope I may die?" demanded Froggie.

"Cross my heart and hope I may die," he repeated solemnly.

Just then an amazed gasp at the door an-

nounced the arrival of one of the teachers.
She took one look and fled to inform the principal. With anxious interest the three boys
sat there awaiting developments. A moment
later Professor Phillips, looking for all the
world like the ruffed old owl that sat at his
desk, strode into the room followed by the jani-
tor. Hastily he directed the removal of the
offending birds. Froggie Sweeney just could
not help tittering. Angrily the principal
turned on the three boys.

" Come to my room at once," he commanded.

In the majesty of offended dignity he escorted them thither and bade them sit down.

" Wait here until after the morning exercises
are over," he directed, stalking out of the room
and locking the door behind him.

" I know boys," he muttered in the hallway.
" It was those three who did it. They thought
they would divert suspicion from themselves by
being the first to arrive."

Meanwhile the trio sat in the principal's
room, vaguely terrified, wondering curiously
what was going to happen. If they could have
faced the ordeal of the principal's questioning
at once, as they had expected, it would have
been much easier. The longer the agony was

deferred the more appalling the prospect seemed.

Froggie Sweeney began to stir uneasily in his chair. "Come on," he suggested, "let's beat it."

"The door's locked," objected the more timorous Fatty Bullen.

"Let's climb out the window and drop down," said the ever resourceful Froggie. "It ain't much of a drop."

"Limp couldn't make it," objected Fatty, speaking one word for Eddie and two for himself. His avoirdupois did not qualify him as a jumper.

"I could, too, make it," retorted Eddie indignantly.

"Come on, then," said Froggie.

"No," said Eddie firmly. "I'm not going to."

"Why not?" demanded Froggie. "It can't be any worse for us than it is now. He'll fire us all anyhow."

"What for?" asked Eddie, in consternation at the thought. "We haven't done anything."

"Makes no differ," said Froggie, "you'll see. Come on."

" No," said Eddie, " I won't.   I'm going to stay."

" So'm I," decided Fatty.

" You ain't going to squeal? "

" No," said Eddie.   " I agreed not to answer any questions.   I'll keep my 'greement. But I'm not going to run away."

Outvoted, Froggie relapsed into sullen silence.   In Eddie's mind was running the chat he had had with old Jonas a couple of weeks before.   He had made a promise, and he must keep it.   Running away, he felt, would not be according to code.   Having committed himself, he must stay and take the consequences — even if it meant his being suspended or expelled.   Somehow, in spite of Froggie's prediction, he could not bring himself to expect any such punishment.   What had they done? While he communed with himself, footsteps were heard in the hall outside.

" Hist, here he comes," whispered Froggie. " Remember our agreement."

" Sure," breathed Eddie and Fatty, " cross my heart."

Into the room strode the principal, still badly ruffled from the morning's unpleasant occurrences.   He seated himself at his desk and gazed severely at the three culprits arrayed before him. He was positive that in Fatty Bullen and Froggie Sweeney he had the ringleaders in the mischief. He knew them both of old. For Eddie's association with them he found it hard to account. Yet he recalled that only a few days before Miss McGuffey had told him of the ten demerits, and had lamented that she feared the youngest of the Randalls was arriving at "the tough age." Principal Phillips wagged his head sagaciously at the thought. He knew boys. They were all alike, all bad, all inclined to mischief. Of course, Eddie was guilty, he decided, without waiting to hear the evidence.

The inquisition began. "Sweeney," said the principal in his severest manner, "what do you know about this disgraceful affair?"

"I got nothing to say," asserted Froggie, trying to assume an injured air.

"Either you will at once confess your part in this, or I will suspend you for two weeks," the principal announced, his strained temper snapping under the boy's defiance.

Principal and pupil glared at each other. It may be that the human eye can subdue a raging lion; it seldom has much effect on a stubborn boy. Sullenly, half under his breath, Sweeney kept repeating the phrase, " I ain't got nothing to say."

" Very well," snorted Professor Phillips, turning to Fatty.

" And you — Bullen — what have you to say for yourself? "

Though Froggie had faithfully remembered the pact, he had forgotten the formula. Not so with Fatty Bullen. " I decline to answer any questions," he repeated with parrot-like accuracy.

The principal wasted little time with him. " You're suspended for two weeks, too," he announced, turning then to Eddie.

Under most circumstances he would have been disposed to deal gently with the little lame boy. Aside from any natural sympathy to be expected, Eddie's record had hitherto been most excellent. It was to Eddie he was looking now for a confession that would clear up the whole matter. He confidently expected that his first question would bring forth information which would confirm his judgment as to the culprits. Of course, Eddie would betray his comrades. Especially if he went at the boy rough-handed, he would be sure to frighten him into telling everything he knew.

" You, Randall," he commanded, in the same brusque, harsh tone he had used toward the others, " tell me instantly everything you know about this."

Eddie gulped, his knees began knocking together, his mouth and lips went suddenly dry, his voice disappeared somewhere away down in the bottom of his throat. There came a hard lump in his stomach, or maybe it was his heart, his face, too, went white, and in his eyes was pleading terror. The confident principal smiled grimly.

Froggie and Fatty eyed him with sudden apprehension. Thus far their plan had worked well. Was Eddie going to spoil it all by weakening?

Eddie, if the truth must be told, wanted very badly to break the compact. It would be so easy to say respectfully: " I know nothing at all about it, sir. I have no idea who did it." If he did so, he felt certain that all his trouble would be over. On the other hand, if he persisted in keeping to the agreement, he realized that he, too, would be suspended at once, as the others had been.

Suspended! Disgraced! He, Edward Haverford Randall, the star good-conduct pupil of the whole school! What would people think? What would mother say? What would dad say? Somehow it did not trouble him in the least as to what old Jonas would say or would think about it. Whatever happened, old Jonas always seemed to understand.

He pictured himself slinking along the streets, people pointing the finger of scorn at him, and saying: "There goes Limpy Randall. He's been suspended from school."

He pictured his mother's tears. She would be so ashamed of him, and would talk to him about it, as sometimes she talked to Tom and Richard when they had been bad. He just felt that he could not be suspended. Yet there was the agreement. He had promised, "cross my heart," to stand by the others. He must do it. That was according to code.

"Well?" said the principal impatiently.

"I — I —" Eddie began falteringly, then gaining new strength from his firm resolve to keep to the code, he announced firmly, "I decline to answer any questions."

Principal Phillips eyed him in amazement.

He announced firmly, " I decline to answer any questions."
Page 142.

He had expected to encounter no resistance whatever from the wan little cripple. "Suspended," he snapped. "I shall send letters to your parents today, telling them that each of you has been suspended for two weeks. You are to go right home at once. I will send up for your hats and books."

Silently the three of them waited until their school property and their hats were in their possession; silently they permitted the still indignant principal to herd them out of the building, the disconsolate little lame boy leading the ignominious procession. As soon as they were safe around the corner up went Froggie Sweeney's cap in the air.

"Oh, goody!" he cried. "No more school for two weeks."

"Great!" cried Fatty Bullen, with enthusiasm wholly forced. He was not at all certain how his suspension would be viewed by his parents.

Eddie said nothing at all. He slipped quietly away from the others and walked dismally home through the rain. It was different with him: he liked school — and what was mother going to say about it?

He decided to tell her at once and have it

over. " I'm suspended," he burst forth as he hobbled into the house.

" What? " cried Mrs. Randall, hardly believing her ears. If it had been Tom or Richard, especially Richard, it would not have surprised her, but Eddie — it seemed impossible. As she looked into her little son's face, the all-seeing mother-eye read there something of the agony he was suffering, and the mother-heart realized how keenly he was feeling the disgrace. " Tell mother all about it," she said quite calmly, gathering him into her lap.

There Eddie quickly sobbed out the whole story, growing more and more comforted as he felt the loving arms drawing him closer and closer. Having finished his tale, he anxiously awaited mother's verdict.

" Well, Eddie, dear," she counseled, " don't worry any more about it now. We'll talk it over with your father tonight and see what he says. I don't think it was fair to send you home for something you didn't do or didn't know anything about. If you have to stay suspended, mother'll help you at home with your lessons so that you will not get behind."

That evening Mrs. Randall told her husband

all about it, waxing indignant as she recited how unfair the principal had been in suspending Eddie. "He hadn't done anything and didn't know who did do it. He was suspended just because he wouldn't tattle, and I don't think it's fair or right."

Mr. Randall only laughed. "Eddie is some kid," he said admiringly; "there's nothing of the quitter about him. Let him stay suspended. It will do him good. I was suspended once myself."

Mrs. Randall shook her head sadly. "There are times," she observed plaintively, "when I just can't understand you, or Eddie either."

"I suppose not," said Mr. Randall indifferently, picking up the evening paper.

Two weeks later the trio of culprits returned to school. At noon they were comparing notes.

"Say, what do you think?" asked Froggie Sweeney indignantly. "Old Phillips found out last week that it wasn't us at all, that it was Ed Gross and his gang that done it."

"How'd you find out?" asked Fatty Bullen.

"Jimmy Flinn heard him telling one of the teachers."

"Gee!" exclaimed Fatty with an aggrieved air, "and he let us stay suspended just the same. Ain't he the mean old thing?"

Eddie Randall listened in puzzled silence. It did seem mean to him that when Professor Phillips learned the truth he had made no amends to the three already punished. Eddie had not yet learned that other code, the code of grown folk, that when they do make mistakes they must never admit it to youngsters.

CHAPTER SEVEN

A CHANGED AMBITION

"IT'S mighty mean of dad not to let me do it," complained Tom.

"It sure is," agreed Richard.

"I wonder why he wouldn't?" asked Eddie.

The place was the Randall barn. The time was Saturday afternoon. It was raining, which accounted for all three boys being in that particular place at such a time as the afternoon of a holiday. The episode under discussion was Hen Ross's quitting school to drive a wagon for the steam laundry.

"He's to get twenty dollars a month for doin' it," continued Tom in an aggrieved manner. "An' he says they'll need another boy Monday, and he could have got the job for me as easy as not."

"Twenty dollars!" exclaimed Dick. "My, that's a lot!" He was silent for a moment or two as he tried vainly to conjecture the purchasing possibilities of such an amount. "Did you tell dad about the money?"

" Sure I did," Tom answered, " an' he just laughed an' said he guessed he could earn enough for the family for a few years yet."

" Did you tell mother about it? " asked Eddie.

" Naw, of course I didn't. Women always want a fellow to keep on going to school."

" Does Hen Ross drive the wagon all by himself? " questioned Eddie.

" No," admitted Tom reluctantly. " That is, not yet. There's a man on the wagon with him. You see, he's got to learn the route first."

" Twenty dollars is a lot of money," sighed Richard.

" It sure is," said Tom. " And dad needs money, too. I heard him and mother talking last night about taking Limpy to New York to see some big doctor and see if he couldn't be cured, and dad said he could not afford it yet."

The red of shame crept into little Eddie's cheeks. It hurt so when Tom or Dick thoughtlessly called him " Limpy." It was bad enough to go through life wearing a heavy iron brace on his leg, bitter enough not to be able to run and jump and swim, terrible enough to be always left at home when the other boys went off on fishing and nutting expeditions. Surely it was punishment enough to have such a lot, to limp when you walked, to be always picked last when they were choosing sides, never to be able to do ever so many things other boys did, without having your own big brother call you by the hated name of " Limpy." The tears all but welled up in his eyes, and a great lump came into his throat.

Tom, however, was too full of his own troubles to notice the anguish his careless epithet had caused Eddie.

" Never mind," he said boastfully, " just you wait a couple of years and watch me.   I'll be sixteen then, and I'm going to run away."

" You're not, really? " breathed Richard enviously.

" I just am, and I'll make a lot of money, too."

" What are you going to do? " asked Eddie, who was in many respects the most practical member of the trio.

" I'm going to be a railroad conductor. They travel everywhere and see everything, and it never costs them a cent.   They get big wages, too.   Nick Dolan's father's a conductor, and he gets seventy-five or eighty dollars a month.   Nick told me so.   By and by he's going to get an express run, and then he'll get more, maybe a hundred dollars. Think of that."

" Oh, pooh," said Richard, " being a conductor's no fun. They just go back and forth between the same places all the time and walk through the trains. I'm going to be a drummer. You get to travel everywhere and have a lot more fun. What are you going to be, Eddie? "

A gleam of ambition lightened the youngest boy's face. He knew well what he wanted to be. His mind had long been made up. A martial soul dwelt in his puny body.

" I'm going to be a soldier, a great general," he announced.

" Pooh," Dick snickered derisively, " you can't ever be a general. They have to ride horses and lead charges. You never could get up on a horse. You're too lame."

Again the red crept into Eddie's face. Bravely he swallowed back his tears. " Too lame " always interfered with all his pleasures and ambitions. However, if he could not be a general, he had other strings to his bow.

" Well, then," he said almost defiantly, " I'm going to be a missionary to Japan."

Tom and Richard eyed him curiously.   In all their plans for the future neither of them had ever conceived any occupation that would take them to such a far-off place.   Japan to them was little more than a name in the geography.   Eddie, as it happened, had been reading a Sunday-school book written by a missionary about Japan, and the story he read there of the quaint costumes and curious habits of the people had fascinated him beyond measure.

"I could be a missionary, couldn't I, Tom?" he asked anxiously.

"I don't know," said Tom dubiously. "You'd have to travel a lot and maybe walk a lot."

"'Course he couldn't," added Richard, "he's too lame.   There's mighty little lame fellows can do."

"I'm not too lame.   I will be a missionary," cried Eddie despairingly, as he fled through the rain to the house.   It was a habit of his, whenever people began to talk about his lameness, to get out of the way.   He just could not stand it to have his infirmity discussed even by the members of his own family.

Once safe in the house, he found his beloved book about Japan and settled himself on the dining-room lounge to reread it, this time from a new view-point. He tried with each page to put himself in the missionary's place, to picture himself doing the things the missionary had done. Only once was he discouraged, as he came to a chapter in which a painful pilgrimage up a steep mountain-side to visit a sacred shrine was described.

" Maybe I couldn't do that," he sighed, " but I don't believe I'm too lame to go as a missionary. I'll ask mother tonight."

All through supper and the rest of the evening he had a splendid time depicting mentally his adventures as a missionary, and was so silent about it that his mother grew worried. Several times she looked anxiously at him, and was about to ask if he wasn't feeling well, but each time she decided to let him alone. As she came up to his bedroom to kiss him good night and to massage his leg, she felt his forehead anxiously for signs of fever, for his cheeks were flushed, and his eyes were sparkling with what seemed to her unnatural brightness.

" Mother," he began, " did you ever hear of a lame missionary? "

" What a funny question! No, I don't think I ever did."

"Do you think I'm too lame to be a missionary?"

"Oh, no indeed," she replied quickly. "You're not so very lame now."

"But," he persisted, "supposing I went to Japan?"

"No, of course not. You could go anywhere as well as any one else."

"What does a missionary have to do?"

Mrs. Randall never lost an opportunity to impress a lesson on her sons.

"A missionary," she explained, "is a man who is very, very good, so that he can teach other people how to be good."

"Am I good enough to be a missionary?"

"Yes," said his mother, "you are a very good boy. If you keep on being good, some day you may become a missionary."

"Well," announced Eddie with conviction, "I'm going to be just as good as I can be, and when I grow up, I'm going to go as a missionary to Japan. Dick said I was too lame, but I'll show him."

"Richard must not say things like that," said his mother as she kissed him good night.

As she went down-stairs to rejoin her husband, she found herself rejoicing at her small

son's announcement. The daughter of a
clergyman, and of a devout temperament, one
of her fondest hopes was that one of her sons
might be a minister.   Neither Tom nor Richard had thus far shown any inclinations in that
direction, or had otherwise given evidence of
any signs of early piety.   That Eddie at ten
should announce his vocation as a missionary
filled her with delight.

"What do you think Eddie told me tonight?" she said to Mr. Randall.   "He announced that when he grew up, he was going to
be a missionary to Japan."

"Boys get funny notions," said Mr. Randall
carelessly.   "He'll   get   over   it   quickly
enough."

"I don't think he will.   He is very serious
about it."

"Oh, pooh," laughed his father, "at his age,
my highest ambition was to be a telegraph line-
man."

"This seems to be his heart's desire," his
mother persisted.   "I'm sure he means it."

The next day, Sunday, Eddie arose with a
fixed determination to begin a new life.
Henceforth he was going to be good, to keep on
getting better and better, until perhaps by and

by he would be as good as the minister, good
enough to be a missionary.

After breakfast he seated himself in the dining-room and began conscientiously to study
his Sunday-school lesson. He tried his best
to keep his thoughts on the leaflet before him,
but quickly found that being persistently good
was no easy task. Out on the porch, through
the open window, he could hear Tom and Richard talking.

"Oh, Tom, lookee what I got."

"Let's see."

"Watch out, or he'll get away."

"Gee, isn't he a dandy? Where'd you get
him?"

Though Eddie kept repeating the text over
and over again, he could not help hearing them.
What was it Richard had found, he wondered.
It must be a butterfly, or a bug, or maybe an
animal of some sort. Maybe it was a turtle.
Curiosity almost overcame him.

"Come on, Dick, let's take him out to the
barn."

"We ought to put him in water, oughtn't
we?"

It must be a turtle, Eddie decided. He
wondered how big it was. He debated with

himself whether it would be very wrong for
him to take a peek at it. No, he decided, he
was going to be good. He was going to keep
on studying his Sunday-school lesson. He had
to learn how to be good enough to be a missionary —

" Tell you what, we'll put him in a barrel
out in the barn so he can't get away, and after
Sunday-school we'll fix him up."

" All right, come on."

It was harder and harder for Eddie to keep
his mind fixed on his text. He wanted so
much to run out to the barn before he started
for Sunday-school and see what they had there,
but somehow he managed to keep from doing
it. Yet all through the morning exercises his
mind wandered. When the teacher called on
him to recite his text, he could not for the life
of him remember the last half of it. All the
time he kept thinking that whatever it was in
the barrel might get away before he had a
chance to see it. In the church service that
followed, he found it difficult to be attentive.
Before setting out that morning he had made
up his mind to listen to everything the minister
said and to watch everything he did. A missionary was a minister. If he was going to go

to Japan, he would first have to learn to be a minister. But somehow, between the turtle and Japan, he forgot all about listening to the minister.

On the way home he tried to remember what the sermon had been about. He was horrified at himself when he found that he could not re-call even the text. He felt utterly dismayed. He doubted whether he could ever learn to like Sunday-school and church enough, whether he could ever be good enough. He decided to ask old Jonas that afternoon what he thought about it.

Meanwhile, Mrs. Randall, walking home from church with two of her neighbors, was proudly telling them of Eddie's new ambi-tion.

"He's very much in earnest about it," she explained. "His father doesn't take him seri-ously, but he never understood Eddie. I am confident he means it, and I'm so delighted!"

"Isn't he a dear?" said one of the women. "He's always such a good, obedient boy I'm sure he'll grow into a good man."

"Yes," said Mrs. Randall, "Eddie never has caused me a minute's worry. He always does just what I tell him and always keeps any promises he makes. He's so different from the other boys."

Dinner that afternoon was not over until three o'clock, and immediately afterward Eddie set out to visit old Jonas. Though the veteran's shop was closed Sundays, Eddie knew from past experience that he would be sure to find him propped up on the sidewalk in front of it, the same as on week-days.

" Don't be gone more than an hour, Eddie dear," his mother said as he started out.

" No'm, I won't," he answered obediently.

Ordinarily Mrs. Randall did not approve of her boys running about the town Sunday afternoons, but she made an exception in Eddie's case, for she felt that he was always to be trusted. She knew of his friendship for the old cripple and rather approved of it, for the daily visits Eddie made gave him something to do. Tom and Richard, on the contrary, always had orders on Sunday afternoon to stay in their own yard.

Soon Eddie, squatted down on an old box where he could look up into Jonas's face, was setting forth his troubles in trying to be good.

" Do you think I could ever get to be good

enough to be a missionary?" he inquired anxiously.

"Sure you could," declared old Jonas.

"I'm afraid not," said Eddie dubiously.
"This is the very first day I've tried it, and it is
going to be pretty hard work."

"Yes," Jonas admitted, "it's likely to be."

"You see, Tom and Richard had something
out on the porch while I was studying my text
— I think it was a turtle — and I wanted to go
out to see what it was —"

"Didn't ye go?"

"No, but I wanted to, and mother says
when you want to do something you oughtn't
to do, it's wrong, almost as wrong as if you
did it."

"How'd you know you'd oughtn't to look
at the turtle?"

"Why," stammered Eddie, "I'm going to
be a missionary, and that means being good all
the time and studying texts and reading the
Bible and —"

"I ain't so sure about that," interrupted
Jonas. "There's lots of people as is pretty
good that don't spend much time reading the
Bible. 'Tisn't what you read, it's what you
do and think that makes you good."

" Wouldn't it have been wrong for me to have gone out to see the turtle when I was studying my text? "

" 'Course it wouldn't.   It's only natural for a boy to want to see a turtle — Sunday or any other day."

" But oughtn't I to study texts and to read the Bible? "

" Sure you ought, but there's time enough for that later.   It's a boy's business to run and jump and play and get all the exercise he can so that he'll grow up into a big, healthy man. It's a boy's business, too, to find out everything he can about everything, including turtles. Them that reads the most ain't always the best and the wisest.   The same One that made the Bible made everything else in the world, and it's just as much of a duty to study one as 'tother."

" I never thought about it like that," said Eddie soberly. " I supposed we learned everything out of books."

" Play's a good thing for boys, yes, and for men, too," continued Jonas. " It's just as natural for a boy to want to play on Sunday as on other days."

" But," exclaimed Eddie, in horrified tones,

"you don't think it's right to play on Sundays, to play games and things?"

"Yes and no," said Jonas. "It's perfectly natural for a boy to want to play seven days a week, but the rules of most parents is he mustn't play Sundays. It's a good thing for a boy to learn to obey rules, for all his life long he's got to be keeping rules. The sooner he learns it the better he'll get along."

"Grownup people," protested Eddie, "don't have to obey any rules. They can do just as they please."

"No indeed, they can't. Everybody has got to obey rules of some sort. There's the rules of the city and state. Grownup people have to obey them or go to jail. They have to do certain things and pay taxes and things like that. Then there's the rules of health; everybody's got to obey them, or they get sick and die. There's the rules of business; a man's got to obey them, or else he fails, or can't get any one to give him any credit. There's the rules of society; everybody's got to keep them, or nobody'll associate with him. Everybody on earth's got to keep some sort of rules as long as he lives."

"I s'pose it's so," sighed Eddie, "but I

always thought that when I grew up I could do just as I pleased."

For a moment there was silence between them, each thinking his own thoughts, old Jonas's reverting to the many things he had wanted to do, but which rules had interfered with, while Eddie tried to digest this new theory of life. It was Eddie who spoke first.

" Mr. Jonas," he asked, " do you s'pose I'll ever be able to earn money — a lot of money? "

" You never can tell till you try. When I was left with one leg —"

" With a leg and a half," interrupted Eddie.

"— I didn't see how I was going to earn much money, but I got this little place here, and I've done pretty well and have some put aside, too. But what do you want to earn money for? "

" There's a doctor in New York I've heard dad and mother talking about. Maybe he could cure me so I wouldn't be lame, but it would cost a lot, and dad can't afford it yet. Maybe, if I could earn enough money, I wouldn't have to be lame any more."

In the boy's eager, upturned face old Jonas with sympathizing eyes read something of the agonized longing — the longing to be like other boys. Well he knew, too, the suffering of going through life physically handicapped, forever hampered and hindered from doing most of the things he wanted to do. Even against his better judgment he answered quickly: " 'Course you can earn money — a lot of money. Any boy can. All you have to do is to keep your eyes open and jump at the first chance that comes along."

Eddie's eyes sparkled with delight at these words of encouragement. A dozen more questions trembled on his lips, but just then two other cronies of Jonas — two old soldiers — came along, to have a Sunday afternoon chat with the veteran, and all opportunity for further confidence was cut off.

Eddie listened for a while to their conversation, and then set out for home, remarking politely, " I guess I'd better be going now."

As he came to the first cross street, a narrow lane that led down the hill to the grove by the railroad tracks, the sound of a band caught his ear. He stopped to look and listen. Down in the grove all sorts of exciting and interesting things seemed to be going on. He could see the canvas tops of tents, could hear the band and, mingling with it, the harsher music of a merry-go-round.

It came to him that he had promised to be home in an hour, but he recalled that his visit had been cut short and decided that he would have a few minutes still, time enough to go down to the end of the street and see what was going on.

As he hobbled down the hill, a great streamer above the entrance to the grove came into view. It announced that the annual picnic of the United Knights of Work was going on there. Around the entrance all sorts of interesting-looking booths had been erected. Through the fence he caught a glimpse of a platform on which he could see couples dancing.

All thoughts of home vanished. Forgotten was his promise to his mother. He felt that he just must get closer to see and hear what was going on. He wanted to find out who the United Knights of Work were. He hobbled faster and faster toward the grove, and before he fully realized it found himself inside the entrance.

" Hey, kid, come here! "

He paused and looked around. The man

who had hailed him was leaning out of a little stand, in which were a lot of holes filled with canes of many designs. The man, both his hands full of small wooden rings, was beckoning to him. Eddie hobbled closer to see what was wanted.

"Say, kid," said the man in a hoarse voice, "do you want to earn a quarter?"

To earn a quarter!

What was it old Jonas had said —"all that a boy has to do is to grab the first chance that comes along"? Forgotten instantly was the fact that it was Sunday, forgotten his promise to be home within an hour, forgotten everything except that here was a chance to prove that despite his lameness he could earn money, that he could earn a quarter — a whole quarter.

"Sure," he said with earnestness.

"Come on, then," said the man. "Get in here and run this stand while I go get something to eat. The rings is three for a nickel. Any fellow that gets one over a cane gets the cane. All you got to do is to keep yelling good and loud to keep the crowd coming and to gather up the rings and take in the money. My voice is wore out."

It was not until supper-time that any of the family noted Eddie's absence.

"Where's Eddie?" asked Mrs. Randall as Tom and Richard came in from the barn where they had had a busy afternoon playing with the turtle. They had no worries about being good. They weren't going to be ministers or missionaries.

"Don't know," said Tom carelessly. "Haven't seen him all afternoon."

"Have you seen Eddie?" Mrs. Randall asked her husband anxiously as he joined them a moment later.

He had no idea where Eddie might be. Mrs. Randall tried in vain to think where he might have gone. She recalled that she had not seen him since early in the afternoon when he set out to call on old Jonas. He must have come home from there long ago. He was to stay only an hour, and he always kept his promises. Perhaps he had gone up to his room or to the attic and had fallen asleep. She went to the foot of the stairs and called and called again. Getting no response, she made a hasty search of the house.

"Where do you suppose Eddie can be?" she asked her husband with blanching face, fearful lest some accident might have befallen her best loved.

"Probably he's over next door playing with Floribel Finch," suggested Mr. Randall. "Tom, you run over and see."

As Tom returned with the news that no one there had seen Eddie, Mr. Randall began to catch a little of his wife's anxiety. Each of the boys was dispatched to the homes of various friends in the neighborhood, but each returned soon with no news of the missing one.

"Where'd you see him last?" asked Mr. Randall.

"About three he went off to see that old man down the street of whom he is so fond," Mrs. Randall answered. "He promised to be back by four. He has never been late before. What can have happened to him?"

"Oh, nothing," said Mr. Randall. "If that is where he is, he has just forgotten all about the time. Time means nothing to a boy. Come on, we'll eat our supper. He'll be home before we're through. An appetite will always bring a youngster home."

It was an uneasy meal to which they sat down. Despite her husband's reassuring words, Mrs. Randall could not eat. A dozen theories formed themselves in her mind as to what might have happened to her little crippled son: maybe he had fallen and hurt himself; perhaps he had been run over; perhaps his brace had slipped, and he was unable to walk. She pictured him lying hurt, perhaps dying, in some neglected neighborhood. She must do something. What was there to do? How could they find him?

As the meal ended without a glimpse of Eddie, her husband, too, grew more and more worried.

"I'll tell you what," he suggested. "You and I'll walk down to the old fellow's place and get Eddie and bring him home. Mind, you two boys stay in the yard while we are gone," he added as a parting injunction to Tom and Richard.

"Do you know the old fellow's name?" Mr. Randall asked his wife as they hurried down the street.

"It's Jonas something, and he's one-legged," Mrs. Randall answered, "but I've never seen him."

With this description Mr. Randall had no difficulty in locating the tobacco-shop, and there in front of it old Jonas was still sitting.

"Have you seen our Eddie?" the mother anxiously asked as they approached.

"Eddie Randall, you mean? Why, yes, he was here this afternoon."

"What time did he leave?"

"Where did he go?"

Both parents spoke at once.

"Let's see," said the old man slowly, "he came about three and he must have stayed till half-past or maybe a quarter of four."

"Which way did he go?"

"Why," said Jonas in surprise, "he went home, of course. He always does. What's happened?"

"It's nearly eight now, and he isn't home yet," Mrs. Randall answered. "He didn't say anything about going anywhere else, did he?"

"Yes and no. He was talking some of going to Japan, but I don't believe he intended starting for there this afternoon."

With growing anxiety the Randalls turned their steps toward home.

"Do you know," said Mrs. Randall with sudden conviction, "I believe Eddie must have run away. I think he has set out for Japan. Ever since yesterday he has been thinking of nothing except going there as a missionary."

"Oh, pooh!" replied her husband. "He's forgotten all about that by now. He just gets those notions like all boys."

"Eddie isn't like other boys," protested his mother. "He's so good. His whole mind and heart have been set on being a missionary. He's been reading his Bible and studying his Sunday-school lesson —"

"Let's turn down here," said Mr. Randall irrelevantly. His ear had caught the sound of a band, and down in the grove he, too, could see the tents.

"There's no use in our looking for Eddie in a place like this," protested Mrs. Randall as they entered the picnic grounds. "It was Eddie's heart's desire to grow up to be a good man, to be a missionary — Well! did you ever?"

There, right in front of her, in plain view under the light of a flaring torch, was her missing son, the would-be missionary, both hands full of wooden rings.

"Come on here!" he was shouting at the top of his shrill little voice. "Get your canes! Take a chance on the canes! Three throws for a nickel! Get your canes!"

Mr. Randall's relief at finding Eddie found

expression in a hearty laugh, and as he stood there gleefully watching his small son's efforts, he was not without some feeling of pride. It was his secret fear that his wife was bringing up their boys to be mollycoddles.

The feeling of Eddie's mother, however, was not delight. Straight for the stand she sped, and, grasping her son's arm, she gave him an indignant shake, spilling rings all over the place.

"Eddie Randall, you naughty boy," she almost screamed at him. "What are you doing here? On Sunday, too! Aren't you ashamed of yourself, disgracing us like this?"

"Oh, mother," cried Eddie jubilantly, her reproaches rolling off like rain-drops, "I earned a quarter running the stand while the man went to supper, and I did so well and made so much money for him he said he'd give me another quarter if I stayed till eight o'clock."

"Eddie Randall," commanded his mother, still holding his arm, "you drop those dirty rings and come right home."

Resolutely he shook off her hand.

"I can't leave till the man comes back," he announced, "and mother, he says if I'll go with

him every day to fairs and picnics, he'll give
me fifty cents a day. I can go, can't I,
mother?" And then, for the first time not-
ing his father's presence and reading in his face
more sympathy and understanding, "I can,
can't I, Dad?"

"But, Eddie," laughed his father, "I
thought you wanted to be a missionary."

All at once the memory of his good resolves
swept over Eddie — his firm intention of being
good all the time, of reading the Bible lots and
lots, of becoming as good as the minister — and
here he was, his promise to be home broken,
selling chances on canes at a Sunday picnic.
He knew he ought to feel ashamed of himself.
He realized that his present occupation fell far
short in fitting him for a missionary career.
He knew he ought to say he was sorry, but he
wasn't sorry a bit. His cheeks flushed. His
voice faltered.

"Aw, that was yesterday," he said.

CHAPTER EIGHT

COUSIN JIM

"BOYS," said Mrs. Randall, as the family gathered at the supper table a few nights later, "I have a surprise for you. See if you can guess what it is!"

"It's a picnic," said Tom.

"It's a peach shortcake," said Richard, always thinking of good things to eat.

"Presents," said Eddie, who liked presents.

"You're all wrong," their mother announced. "Your Cousin Jim is coming to visit us."

If she had anticipated that her announcement would be received with enthusiastic acclaim, she was doomed to disappointment. Instead she became at once the center of a volley of questions.

"When's he coming?" demanded Richard.

"How old is he?" Tom wanted to know.

"Where'll he sleep?" asked Eddie.

"How long's he going to stay?"

"Is he bigger'n me?"

" Is Aunt Margaret coming with him? "

" How'd you know he was coming? "

" Wait, boys," she directed. " I can't answer all your questions at once. Wait and I will tell you everything. He is coming next Thursday to stay for two weeks. Your Uncle Jim is going through to Chicago, and will bring Jim with him. He will stop off for a day on his way back, and take your cousin home, so Aunt Margaret's letter says."

" How old is he? " persisted Tom.

He was fourteen, the eldest. Eddie, the lame duck of the Randall trio, was ten. Richard came half-way between them.

" Let me see," said their mother. " Jim was born just a month after Richard. That makes him not quite twelve."

" Oh," said Tom, in a disappointed tone, " he's a little fellow."

" Sure," said Richard, " he's a little fellow. He's younger'n me."

" What's he like? " asked Eddie, rejoicing at the thought that he was to have a new playmate.

" I haven't seen Jim since he was two years old," their mother explained. " He was a beautiful baby, so sturdy and so strong. It was just after Eddie was born that Aunt Margaret came to visit us, and brought him with her."

" He hasn't any brothers or sisters, has he? " questioned Eddie.

" No, he's an only child; so you boys must all be nice to him and show him how lovely it is to have brothers."

" He'll have to sleep with Eddie," Tom announced. " There ain't any room for him in with Dick and me."

" There isn't any room," his mother corrected.

" That'll be fine," announced Eddie, to his mother's satisfaction.

Mrs. Randall had been wondering what they would do about sleeping arrangements. They had no spare room. She had been wondering whether her little lame son would welcome a roommate. He was such a quiet reserved chap, so different from the other boys. The iron brace he had to wear constantly on one leg handicapped him so much in the things that other boys liked to do that he had invented all sorts of amusements and recreations of his own. She had not felt at all certain that he would like having a bed companion. But his ready acquiescence in his older brother's suggestion solved the problem.

" You boys must always remember that he is company, and must let him play with your things, and introduce him to all your play-mates," Mrs. Randall continued.

" I can't be bothered trailing round with a kid like that," Tom announced with an almost defiant air.

" I'll bet I can lick him," announced Richard.

" Why, Richard! " his mother exclaimed, " you mustn't say things like that."

Mr. Randall laughed. " Better size him up first, Dick," he suggested. About a year before he had spent a day in Cousin's Jim's home, and he had a vague recollection that his nephew was quite a big boy for his age, bigger even than Tom, despite being two years his junior.

" I do hope our boys will not quarrel with Jim," said Mrs. Randall despondently, as she and her husband still sat at table after their sons had been excused. " I know Margaret must have brought her boy up nicely."

" I guess Jim can take care of himself," said Mr. Randall indifferently. " I know our boys can — at least Tom and Richard can."

"It is them I am worrying about," his wife answered. "Eddie is such a dear good little fellow, I can trust him. I know that he and Jim will get along well together. Eddie is such an obedient boy, I always feel I need not worry about him."

"He did run away once," suggested her husband, chuckling.

Somehow Mrs. Randall never could quite grasp her husband's view-point where the boys were concerned; at times it seemed to her that he fairly gloried in their misdeeds.

"Eddie didn't mean to run away that time," she retorted, ever rising quickly to the defense of her youngest. "His intention was the best. He only wanted to earn some money."

"Boys' intentions always are all right," her husband persisted. "It's their lack of judgment that gets them into trouble."

"Well, Eddie, I know, will get along well with his cousin."

"We'll see," said her husband. "You never can tell about boys."

"But I don't know about Tom and Richard," Mrs. Randall persisted. "They are so rough and rude at times. I am afraid they will spoil Margaret's boy. She always had such

high ideals of motherhood, and with only one
child to look after, she has had lots of time to
devote to him. I suppose her son will be a perfect little gentleman. Our two older boys are
so impolite. They fight and use slang. Yes,
and they both tell fibs, too. I don't think they
really mean to lie, but they are not always
truthful. I am so discouraged about them."

"All boys do that sort of thing. It's boy
nature," said Mr. Randall carelessly.

"I'm sure Margaret's boy will not be like
that," insisted his wife. "My sister's son, I
know, will have had wise and careful bringing
up. Margaret never was as easy-going as I
am."

"The kind of a mother my boys have suits
me exactly," said Mr. Randall, giving her a
little peck on the cheek, as he got up from the
table. "These strict women with ideals and
theories seldom make good mothers. And
don't go worrying your head about Jim's good
manners. No boy of twelve ever has any."

Three days later Cousin Jim arrived, a great
gangling hulk of a boy, all hands and feet, with
a freckled face, mischievous eyes, and a shock
of red hair that simply would not stay brushed.
Tom, straightening himself up to the full height

of his fourteen years, noted with dismay and a sudden feeling of helpless wrath that his cousin was fully two inches taller than he. Richard, the pugnacious, secretly studied Jim's muscular development and decided to await further eventualities before he tried to "lick" him. Only Eddie was politely and effusively cordial.

During the ten minutes after Jim's arrival, while Mr. and Mrs. Randall were present to greet their nephew, the attitude of the boys toward one another, as is generally the case of all boys with strangers, was one of frigid indifference. After Jim's bag had been taken upstairs to Eddie's room, after inquiries about Jim's father and mother and his progress in school had been answered more or less satisfactorily, Mrs. Randall bade the four of them run out into the yard, and play. As soon as they were safely out of the door, Tom hastened away.

"Got to go over and see Bob Tucker," was the only explanation he vouchsafed.

"I'm going with you," said Richard, hastening to follow.

Neither of them showed the slightest expectation or wish to have Cousin Jim accompany them. Eddie stood stock-still, amazed at and ashamed of his brothers' lack of courtesy toward their guest.

Jim didn't seem to mind it in the least. He looked about the yard until he had found a stone, and sent it hurtling after them. It just missed Richard's leg, and Eddie breathed a sigh of relief. Jim gave a grunt of disappointment, and, looking about for another missile but failing to find one, turned to inspect Eddie.

" Come on, old one-leg," he said, " an' we'll have some fun."

Any reference to his deformity, especially from a stranger, always upset Eddie. At his cousin's brutal remark about his iron-braced leg he wanted to turn and run into the house, but duty toward a guest forbade, especially after his brothers' conduct.

" I'm not a one-leg," he protested bravely, mustering up courage enough for a forced smile, and recalling the joke that he and old Jonas, the one-legged veteran, had between them, he added, " I'm a leg and a half, you — you — you redhead."

" All right, leg and a half," laughed Jim, to Eddie's surprise not in the least perturbed by the reference to his hair. " Come on, let's go out to the barn and have some fun."

"Sure," said Eddie, recovering his composure, and deciding that Cousin Jim wasn't such a bad fellow after all.

No sooner had the barn-door swung to behind them than Jim brought forth from his pocket a package of cigarettes and some matches. Ceremoniously lighting one, he offered another to the astounded Eddie, who hardly knew what to make of the performance. Why, even Tom, who was fourteen, never had dared to try to smoke yet.

"Let them fellers go their own way," announced Jim, "you and me'll be pals and have a lot of fun. Tell you what, old one-leg, we'll organize a pirate band and have a secret oath, just us two."

"Gee, that'll be great," cried Eddie with kindling eyes. Here was a playmate after his own heart. Tom and Richard lacked imagination and never would play the pretend games he enjoyed so much.

"I'll be Captain Kidd," continued Jim, "and you be Peg-leg, the sailor. Are you game?"

"Sure I'm game," asserted Eddie. Of course he was. Hadn't Brother Tom declared

more than once that Eddie was a " game little
kid "?

" Then stand up," commanded Captain
Kidd, " and say the pirates' oath."

Slowly he repeated the words, Eddie
solemnly saying them after him, " Sticks and
stones, blood and bones, I swear to keep the
secrets of the band, and if I don't, I hope to die
and to be drawn and quartered and hung at the
yard-arm."

" Now," announced Captain Kidd, " we're
blood-brothers.   We dassent ever tell on each
other, and we share the loot.   See what I got."

From his pocket he produced a new ten-dol-
lar bill.

" Where'd you get all that money? " cried
Eddie in amazement.

" Copped it out of Dad's pocket last night in
the sleeping-car," boasted Jim.

" But's that's stealing," protested the horrified Eddie.

" Sure it is," assented Jim.   " That's what
pirates do.   They steal and kill and rob and
burn."

" I don't believe I want to be a pirate, if
you'll excuse me," said Eddie timorously, after
a moment's thought.

"It's too late now, you've got to be," announced the pirate captain. "You've taken the oath. You can't go back on that, you'd be stricken dead if you did. You don't want to die, do you?"

"No," said Eddie. He was sadly perplexed. He wished he could ask old Jonas what to do. Jonas said a man always had to keep his word. Surely it was more important to keep an oath. He had taken his oath to be a pirate. He couldn't see any way out of it.

"All right," he said, "I'll keep my oath. I'll be a pirate."

"Hurrah for Peg-leg," shouted Captain Kidd. "Come on, then, we'll go in search of loot."

Arming himself with a barrel stave, and carelessly tossing his cigarette, which had fortunately gone out, into a pile of hay, he led the way outdoors. Out behind the barn they encountered four sleek white ducks placidly waddling along in search of worms.

"Ahoy, there, Peg-leg," cried the captain gleefully, "stand by to capture the enemy."

"They're not our ducks," protested Eddie. "They belong to the Widow Malone who lives over there."

" We'll capture 'em anyway," directed Captain Kidd.

Whatever scruples Eddie may have felt, he soon forgot them in the fascinating sport of driving the unwilling ducks into the barn, where Jim quickly closed the door behind them to prevent their escape.

" Now," he said gleefully, " if we only had a fire, we'd roast them and have a pirate feast."

" Dad wouldn't let us ever have a fire in the barn," explained Eddie. " It's too dangerous. He doesn't even like us to build a fire anywhere in the yard unless he's around."

Jim, however, hardly heard him. His fertile brain was already busy with another project. He had spied an ax lying beside the kindling block.

" Tell you what we'll do," he announced. " We'll hold a court and try 'em for treason, and if we find they're guilty, we'll behead them."

" Fine," said Eddie. He hadn't seen the ax. He thought it was to be only a pretend execution. Being a pirate was lots of fun.

Cousin Jim, however, was thorough-going in his methods. Before the horrified Eddie had quite realized what was happening the headless

body of one of the ducks was tumbling grotesquely about the barn-floor.

"Oh, stop," cried Eddie. "You've killed
it."

"Sure," grinned Jim cheerfully, "that's
what pirates always do to their captives."

"Dad'll be awful angry," warned Eddie.

"Who'll tell him?" demanded the execu-
tioner unperturbed. "You dassent. You
dassent break your pirates' oath." Forthwith
he began chasing another of the ducks.

"I'm going to tell," jeered a triumphant
voice from the barn-door. It was Richard, returned to see what was going on and snooping
at his cousin's pastime. "I'm going to tell
dad, and you'll get an awful whaling."

"Tattle-tale, tattle-tale," jeered Jim derisively.

"That's all right," scoffed Richard. "Just
wait till I tell on you, and see what you get —
and Eddie, too. That was one of the Widow
Malone's ducks."

"You tell on me," threatened Jim, swagger-
ing toward the door, "and I'll punch your face
off."

"Pooh," said Richard defiantly, feeling perhaps a little overconfident from the fact that he

was in no way involved in the duck killing.
" Who's afraid of you? "

" You are," announced Jim.   " I'll dare and
double-dare you to hit me.   Just you try it
once."

As his cousin advanced, Richard was seized
with sudden misgivings about his ability to
thrash Jim.   Jim was a good deal bigger than
he was.

" I don't fight with fellers younger'n me,"
he announced lamely.

" Fraid-cat and tattle-tale," chanted Jim
mockingly.   " Fraid-cat and tattle-tale."

The double taunt was too much for boy blood
to endure.   With head down and fists clenched
Richard charged at him.   Jim squared off in
an   attitude   of   self-defense.   Unscientific
though the ensuing battle was on either side,
jealousy of the other's prowess lent vigor to
the blows.   Back and forth over the barn-floor
they staggered and tussled, striking wildly at
each other, often clinching in desperate efforts
to throw each other to the floor.

Eddie stood rooted to one spot watching the
combat with impartial, but excited gaze.   He
did not want to see his brother get the worst of
it, but, on the other hand, he felt that as a mem-

ber of the pirate band he would like to see his captain triumph. As the battle raged, he found himself vaguely wishing that he, too, could fight. It must be lots of fun. Yet somewhere in the background of his brain was a vague sense of guilt. What was dad going to say about the duck? What would mother think about the fighting?

By this time both boys' noses were bleeding. Jim's fist caught Richard in the eye with a blinding smack. They clinched and rolled to the floor. At first Richard was uppermost, but soon Jim's superior size and weight prevailed. Both were so out of breath that they could hardly speak.

" Holler 'nuff, and I'll let you up," wheezed the conqueror.

Richard's answer was a last desperate struggle to roll out from under and regain his position of advantage. For a moment they wrestled desperately. At last Jim got his fingers about his opponent's throat.

" Say 'nuff," he commanded again.

" 'Nuff," gurgled Richard.

Slowly they drew apart and scrambled to their feet, eying each other with new sensations of friendship and respect.

" Oh, Dick," shrilled Eddie in alarm, " your eye's getting all black."

" That's nothing," boasted Dick, cautiously feeling the injured eye with his grimy fingers. " I've often had a black eye.   It doesn't hurt." If only he could keep mother from noticing it, he thought, he would have a lot of fun showing it to the fellows tomorrow.

It was just at this juncture that Tom arrived. He viewed the scene of combat with a sinking heart.   It pained him to think that there had been " a dandy scrap," and he had not been there to see it.

" Can't I leave you kids alone five minutes without your getting into a fight? " he demanded loftily.

" You shut up, or I'll fight you too," blustered Jim, perhaps with not quite as much assurance as when he had defied Richard.   He was still badly winded, and, besides, Tom was bigger than Richard.

" I don't fight with children," said Tom with all the bravado of fourteen.

" You're afraid.   You dassent," taunted Jim.

" I dare anything you dare," retorted Tom angrily.

The resourceful Cousin Jim cast about for something to test his oldest cousin's prowess.

"I'll dare you to climb to the top of that ladder there and jump down."

"Pooh, that's nothing," said Tom.

"Dare, dare, double-dare you," repeated Jim.

"Come on, then," retorted Tom, scrambling up the ladder that led to the barn-loft, fully twelve feet higher than the barn-door. Jim quickly followed him up the ladder; Richard, forgetful of his hurts, drew off to one side with Eddie to watch the jumps. At the top of the ladder another controversy took place. Looking down from where they were, the distance seemed far greater than it had from the floor. Both the boys, to tell the truth, were a little afraid of the jump. "Go on and jump," ordered Tom.

"Naw," objected Jim, "you go first. It's your barn."

"You dared me."

"You're afraid."

"I ain't either, you scare-cat."

"I'll show you if I am."

"An' I'll show you. Go on and jump."

"All right, here goes," said Jim.

As he spoke he flung himself down. He lighted safely on his feet, but toppled over, coming to rest uninjured on a pile of hay. The shock of his leap shook him up, but he managed to ejaculate.

" Go on, now, you scare-cat, beat that."

Thus challenged, Tom jumped. He was not so fortunate. As he landed, his foot slipped in the welter of blood left from the execution of the duck. He toppled over with one leg doubled up under him. He gave a shrill scream and fainted. Aghast at the unexpected outcome of the challenge, Jim and Richard ran to his side and tried to straighten out the injured leg, frantically imploring him to speak to them.

Eddie with one glance at his brother's white, senseless face, hobbled out of the barn and made for the house as fast as his lame leg would carry him, shrieking at the top of his voice: " Tom's killed! Tom's killed!"

Mr. Randall happened to be just coming up on the porch. He reached the barn a minute ahead of his wife and Black Maggie, the cook. He carried Tom into the house and laid him on the dining-room sofa. Revived by the motion, Tom opened his eyes and began to moan.

Maggie, without waiting to be told, ran down the street, returning in a few minutes with the doctor.

"Don't worry," said Mr. Randall to his wife. "It's only a broken leg. I had mine broken twice, and you boys," he added, "get out of here and stay out where you won't be in the road."

As soon as the doctor arrived, there was a scurrying through the house, a call for hot water, a rush by Maggie to the drug-store, occasional shrieks of pain from the patient, sobs from Mrs. Randall, the queer, all-pervading odor of antiseptics — and meanwhile, out on the front porch steps sat three small guilty boys, talking in whispers.

"I wonder if he'll die," said Richard. "Do people ever die from broken legs?"

"Naw," said Jim scornfully. "I broke a finger once. It hurt awful, and I had to wear a bandage for ever so long, but that was all."

"Do you s'pose," breathed Eddie anxiously, "that brother Tom'll be lame when he gets well?"

"No," said Richard, "people that are lame are born that way."

"Old Jonas wasn't," replied Eddie. "He lost his leg in battle."

"That's different, of course, but most people that are lame are born that way."

"And they'll never get over it, either," added Jim unfeelingly.

"I guess that's right," said Eddie, gulping down a lump in his throat.

By and by Maggie summoned them into the kitchen for an impromptu supper. Tom, they learned, had been carried up-stairs and put to bed in mother's room and would have to stay there for weeks and weeks. Mother would stay there and nurse him and sleep on the lounge. Dad was to share Richard's bed, and Cousin Jim and Eddie were to sleep together as had been previously arranged.

As they ate their supper, an angry voice was heard at the kitchen-door. It was Mrs. Malone demanding to see Mr. Randall. It took all Maggie's diplomacy to get her away, and after she had gone, Maggie summoned Mr. Randall from up-stairs and held a whispered conference with him in the hall, while the boys listened with misgivings.

"She's found out about the duck," whispered Richard to the pirate leader.

"Don't you dare tell," cautioned Jim; "remember you took the oath."

Eddie nodded assent.

Mr. Randall's face was set and stern as he strode into the kitchen.

"What have you boys been doing with Mrs. Malone's ducks?" he asked, turning with suspicion toward Richard.

"Nothing," said Dick promptly and boldly, fortified by the assurance of innocence.

"Nothing," echoed Jim, equally boldly, fortified by the consciousness of guilt.

Mr. Randall turned to Eddie. "And you, son?"

"Nothing," stammered Eddie, not daring to break his pirates' oath.

"I'll get at the truth of this matter in the morning," announced Mr. Randall, returning to the sick-room up-stairs.

Under the influence of the doctor's powders, Tom had now fallen asleep; so his father began telling his wife about the duck.

"As if we didn't have enough trouble today," he said, "the Widow Malone has just been over to report that she found one of her ducks in our barn with its head cut off. All the boys deny knowing anything about it.

But I'm going to look into the matter further in the morning. Those confounded youngsters must be taught to leave other people's property alone."

"Leave it to me," counseled Mrs. Randall. "I'll get Eddie to tell me how it happened."

But to her utter consternation Eddie absolutely refused to tell her anything. She begged, she pleaded, she threatened, but Eddie remained obdurate. To all her questions he remained at first sullenly silent, and at last tearfully obstinate.

"I can't imagine what has gotten into Eddie," she complained to her husband that night after the boys were all in bed.

"It's the effect of Cousin Jim," Mr. Randall replied. "He's such a perfect little gentleman," he added.

His sarcasm was entirely lost on his wife. "You'll have to take that young ruffian home tomorrow," she announced. "We can't have him around. He hasn't been here a day yet, and he's responsible for Tom breaking his leg, and he blacked Richard's eye, and has made Eddie tell lies. I just will not have him here corrupting our boys."

It was the next day. Father had departed

on the morning train, escorting Cousin Jim home, Tom's broken leg being given as the ostensible reason why Mrs. Randall could no longer have him as a guest. Tom himself, fretful from pain, was keeping his mother busy waiting on him. Richard, lonesome for the companionship of his older brother, and in disgrace over his swollen eye, had made the morning miserable for Eddie by tormenting him.

Eddie, in the black books of both dad and mother because of the fibs he had told in his efforts not to break the pirates' oath, feeling utterly wretched and miserable, had at last escaped from Richard and sought shelter with his friend and counselor, old Jonas, the one-legged veteran. To him he had recounted the complete history of the dire events that had followed Cousin Jim's arrival.

" And I couldn't break my oath, the pirates' oath, could I," he concluded plaintively, " even if I had to fib to dad and mother? "

" Your mistake," advised old Jonas, after pondering while he filled his pipe, " was in following your Cousin Jim into mischief in the first place. You'd ought to have found out what kind of a fellow he was first. You seen him hurl a stone at your own brother, didn't ye? That oughter have warned you to look out for him. It's a good rule, Eddie, all through life, to be pretty certain about a fellow before you tie up with him too close. When you make a new acquaintance, watch every little thing about him. If he has a mean streak in him, it'll soon show in some little thing. It always pays to keep your eye on a strange dog's tail."

" For fear he'll bite? " asked Eddie.

" Yes," said Jonas, " for fear he'll bite."

CHAPTER NINE

A BAD PARTNERSHIP

THE mysterious call of Spring surged in the veins of the Randall boys. It filled them with those strange, exciting, hardly understood longings and desires such as from time immemorial all men have felt, such vernal impulses as have driven whole tribes to migrate, crusaders to go forth crusading, bricklayers to strike, flat-dwellers in the city to buy lots in the suburbs, tramps to take to the road and small boys everywhere to become restless and dissatisfied and devote their energies to devising new pastimes.

"How much money 've you got?" asked Richard of Tom.

"I've got a quarter," Tom replied somewhat suspiciously. "What do you want to know for?"

Only a few minutes before his father had given him the money in payment of an errand done two days ago. It had not been his intention to reveal the possession of this wealth to

either of his brothers. He had secret plans
that involved the spending of the whole amount
without any assistance from either Richard or
Eddie. He felt rather cross with himself for
having let Dick surprise him into telling about
it by his unexpected question.

"'Tain't enough," answered Dick promptly.

"It isn't enough," corrected Tom.

"It isn't enough. I've got fifteen cents myself. It'll take at least a dollar, or maybe a
dollar and a quarter."

"What's the notion?"

Dick looked about to make sure they were
unobserved and took the further precaution of
whispering his idea into his brother's ear.

"Great," cried Tom enthusiastically, "if we
only had the money!"

"We'll get it somehow," said Dick confidently. "Where's Limpy? He's always got
money."

"Reading on the porch, I guess. That's
where he generally is."

"Come on, let's see."

It was quite true that Eddie generally was to
be found on the porch reading. Even though
he could not run and jump, he was far from
being a melancholy youngster. He enjoyed

reading. His imagination was not crippled if his leg was, and in the printed page the youngest of the Randalls participated in far more glorious adventures than did his more active elder brothers.

"Say, Eddie," interrupted Dick, "how much money 've you got?"

Slowly and regretfully Eddie closed his book, marking his place with his finger.

"What do you want to know for?"

Eddie had learned from bitter experience that it was a wise precaution to find out all that was possible about Dick's schemes before committing himself to them.

"I've got a dandy scheme," Dick persisted, as Eddie eyed him dubiously, "but of course if you don't want to go in with Tom and me —"

"Is Tom in it?" questioned Eddie.

"Sure," said Tom, "I'm in it, and if you've got money enough we'll let you be partners with us."

Now that he knew that Dick's plan had brother Tom's approval Eddie felt that he was on safer ground. It was so seldom his brothers let him participate in their affairs that he regarded his opportunity to be partners with them as a great honor.

" I've eighty-nine cents," he announced proudly.

" Bully," said Dick. " That'll be enough. I know where we can get a lamb, a nice little woolly white lamb, for only a dollar and a quarter."

" Oh, great! " cried Eddie, in his enthusiasm dropping his book and losing his place. " Can we really get it? Will mother let us keep it? "

" Sure she will. We'll build a little pen for it out in the barn and we'll take turns feeding it. It won't need much to eat. All lambs eat is a little grass."

" And by and by," said Dick, " when the lamb gets big, we'll sell it and maybe get ten dollars for it."

" Won't that be fine? " said Eddie. He had not even heard what Dick had said about selling the lamb. He had been so busy thinking how nice it would be to have a real live pet to play with. It had been ever so long since they had had any pets. Mother would not have dogs about the place. She said a dog tracked up the porch so. Last year they had had a pair of rabbits. They had taken week about in feeding them but Dick had forgotten when it came his turn and the rabbits had died. Father had said then they were to have no more pets until they had learned how to take care of them. Eddie made up his mind now that whether it was his turn or not he would always see that the lamb got plenty to eat.

"Hurry up," commanded Tom, "get your money and we'll go after it."

Scrambling quickly to his feet Eddie limped hastily upstairs to the chest in which he kept his books and other treasures, returning with three quarters, a dime and four pennies which he surrendered to Tom, as treasurer of the new partnership. Dick, as pilot, led the way to the railroad siding where a flock of sheep was assembled awaiting shipment. An hour before, he had conducted the preliminary negotiations for a lamb, so the deal was quickly concluded.

It was a wabbly-legged little woolly animal with a feeble bleat, but they felt well-satisfied with their purchase and the three of them had a lot of fun getting it home. First they undertook to lead it with a rope around its neck, but the lamb had other notions. Dick tried getting behind and pushing it, but the lamb lay down whenever he attempted this. They gath-

ered grass and leaves and tried luring it on
step by step, but this method of progress
proved too slow to be satisfactory. Eventually
they solved the problem by taking turns in
carrying it. At least Tom and Richard took
turns. When Eddie begged to be allowed to
take the new pet in his arms Dick wouldn't let
him.

" You're too lame," he announced. " You
might stumble with it and it'd get hurt and
die."

After that Eddie did not plead any more to
carry the lamb. He was sensitive about his
lameness, even when his own brothers spoke of
it. His face colored and a lump came into his
throat. Oh, so often it seemed that when there
was anything he wanted to do very much he was
always " too lame." At least he wasn't too
lame to hobble along beside his brothers, from
time to time reaching out his hand to touch the
lamb's little cold nose or to smooth its soft
wool.

" Anyhow the lamb doesn't know I'm lame,"
he consoled himself. " I'll make it like me better than it does Tom and Dick."

Somewhat to their surprise their mother
made no objection to their having this new pet.

Probably she did not foresee any probability of its becoming a habitué of the house.

"Why, boys, where did you get the nice little lamb?" was all she said.

"Down by the railroad track," Tom answered, feeling somewhat relieved when she did not ask how much they had paid for it. He felt sure it was worth a dollar and a quarter but he was not so certain his mother would think so.

"Don't forget to feed it!" she called after them as they took it off to the barn.

For the first day or two the three boys were in a constant wrangle over the lamb. They argued for hours over the selection of a name for it, finally adopting that suggested by Eddie.

"Its wool is sort of reddish about the head," he had remarked, "so let's call it Queen Bess, after the Queen of England. She had red hair."

And Queen Bess the lamb became.

Providing rations for Queen Bess's insatiable appetite at first seemed quite a pleasant pastime. The boys gathered grass and leaves and begged lettuce and cabbage from the cook. They tied Queen Bess to a tree in the yard and watched to see how long it would take her to nibble a bare circle around the tree. The building of a pen in the barn took Tom and Richard nearly the whole day, but soon they began to tire of their new pet.

Queen Bess had too peaceful a disposition to satisfy either the energetic Tom or the bellicose Dick. It was not long before everyone in the household began to refer to Queen Bess as Eddie's lamb. He alone remained faithful in his attendance on the Queen. It was he who fed and watered her. It was he who hurried home from school to shift the tether to another tree before the grass was quite nibbled to the roots.

Jubilantly he informed old Jonas Tucker of the new acquisition.

" So you've got a pet lamb, have you," said old Jonas, chuckling, " all your own! "

" Well, not quite all my own," Eddie explained. " Tom and Dick and I are partners in it."

" So that's it, is it? And I suppose you take turns in feeding it."

" Oh, no," said Eddie, " they're very nice about it. They let me feed it most of the time."

" I'll warrant they do that," said old Jonas
with a fine sarcasm that was, entirely lost on
Eddie.   " Was the lamb given to you? "

" We bought it for a dollar and a quarter.
I put in eighty-nine cents."

" Oh, I see,— so it's mostly yours."

" No," said Eddie, " we all own it.   We're
partners in it.   That's what Brother Tom said.
Don't you understand? "

Old Jonas shook his head sagely.

" You want to watch out for this partner
business, Eddie.   It ain't always such a very
good thing.   You're apt to get the worst of it
when you go partners with any one."

" But these partners are my own brothers,"
Eddie persisted.   " We bought the lamb together and we own it together, don't we? "

" Yes and no.   As long as partners agree
everything's all right but when they have a falling out it is one against one or two against
one and there's the dickens to pay."

" But Tom and Dick are nice partners.
They let me take care of Queen Bess most all
the time.   Why, they even speak of her as
mine."

" All I can say is," cautioned old Jonas,
" watch out for partners.   I went partners

once with a couple of men. I was twelve years paying off their debts."

Yet as the days went by old Jonas's warning seemed wholly uncalled for. Eddie was left in undisputed possession of the new pet. Queen Bess, too, grew very much attached to him and followed him about, pattering after him just like a little white dog. Mrs. Randall learned to her dismay that lambs could track up clean floors and porches with almost as much facility as puppies could. For a while, until his mother put a stop to it, it was no unusual thing to find Eddie reading on the dining-room sofa with the lamb snuggling up to him.

But as time went on Queen Bess, as she grew and grew, seemed to be losing her lamblike peacefulness. She began to exhibit a spirit of aggressiveness and to acquire the habit of leaping lightly out of her pen whenever she found the barn door open, and with three boys in the family open doors were no unusual occurrence.

While Queen Bess was little Eddie gave her a bath almost every day and spent much time in combing out her long white wool. By and by as the novelty wore off and Queen Bess's size made these ablutions more difficult the lamb went practically unwashed and her matted wool was generally full of cinders, detracting greatly from her beauty in the eyes of everyone but Eddie.

One day as Mr. Randall was about to eject Queen Bess from the front porch, he stooped suddenly and ran his hand over the animal's head. Dick noticed that he was chuckling.

"What is it, Dad," he asked. "What's the matter?"

"Eddie's lamb is growing horns," Mr. Randall announced.

"Oh, fellers," shrilled Dick to his brothers, "what do you think? Queen Bess isn't a she. She's a he. Come look!"

The other two boys came running at such a startling announcement and all three of them in turn felt Queen Bess's head to verify the fact discovered by their father. Sure enough there were horns sprouting, two hard little lumps, but unquestionably horns.

"And Queen Bess isn't a nanny lamb at all," cried Eddie in disappointed tones.

"You bet she isn't," said Dick, "She's a billy lamb."

"Oh, shucks," said Tom with the superior knowledge of fourteen, "you don't call sheep

nannies and billies. That's what they call
goats."

" What do they call them then? " demanded
Dick.

" Why," faltered Tom — for the life of him
he could not remember —" they call them —
that is —"

" Bucks and ewes," said his father, coming to
his rescue.

" At any rate," said Tom, " we've got to find
a new name for her.   Tell you what, we'll call
him Pete."

" T'sright," echoed Dick, " Pete it is."

" I don't think that is a nice name," objected
Eddie.   " I am going to call him Sir Walter."

" Nothing doing," insisted Dick.   " His
name is Pete.   I guess he's as much our lamb
as he is yours.   Isn't that right, Tom? "

" Sure it's right," decided Tom.   " We all
three went partners in him.   Dick and I say
his name's to be Pete so that settles it."

" I suppose it does," said Eddie sorrowfully,
his sense of loyalty to his brothers restraining
him from further argument.   He did not like
Pete for a name at all, and after that when he
was alone with the lamb he used to pretend that
Pete was a knight travelling incognito and

then he invariably addressed him as " Sir Walter."

It did not seem to make much difference to Pete by what name he was called. He still continued to follow Eddie around and when he was barred from following his playmate into the house he would make himself at home on the porch until Eddie came out again. Toward others however his disposition continued to grow more aggressive. Once or twice when Black Maggie drove him away from the kitchen door he showed an inclination to resent it. He would lower his head and " baa " at her ominously. On one occasion he even made a rush at her and tried to butt her, but was quickly put to rout with her broom.

"Dat Pete lamb's getting to be a powerful nuisance round here," she complained vociferously to Mrs. Randall.

"I know it, but Eddie loves him so, and the poor little chap has so few pleasures."

"Yas'm, dat's the truf," Maggie would reply, for with all her complaining the Randalls' cook was fond of all three boys and would have been the last person in the world to deprive Eddie of any joy in life. Of the three he was her favorite, for he was far more thoughtful of

others than Dick or Tom, and since the time
that old Jonas had pointed out how much other
people did for him and how little he did for
others he had conscientiously tried to do all the
little services he could each day — that is, he
tried when he didn't forget.

If Pete had only confined his unwelcome at-
tentions to Maggie and the other members of
the Randall family he might have continued in
his career for many months unmolested. Un-
fortunately he was not discriminating.

When the notion seized him Pete would
scamper merrily off to some neighbor's garden
and make a midday meal of the pea vines or
the pansy plants, his sharp little hoofs demol-
ishing almost as much as did his insatiable jaws.
One day, too, in a playful mood he butted
Floribel Finch, arrayed in a clean white slip,
right off the sidewalk into a pool of muddy
water. With the people who lived on all sides
of them the Randalls began to have strained
relations.

The boys of the town, however, began to take
new interest in Pete, as he developed a warlike
spirit. Fatty Bullen with Froggie Sweeney
and Tom and Richard invented a brand new
game with Pete as the star performer.

With an old red cape that had once belonged to Fatty's sister they played bull-fight. They would take turns in wearing the cape and teasing Pete until he would angrily lower his head and charge them. The other boys armed with sharpened sticks would play that they were matadors and drive Pete off. Sometimes the red-caped tormentor would not get out of the way quite quickly enough and would be ignominiously butted over amid the shouts of the comrades. Such mishaps only added to the merriment of the game and caused their mothers to wonder how they managed to tear their clothes in such queer places.

In this sport Eddie took no part. He could not have done so, even if he had wished to, for his iron brace prevented him from running. Furthermore it always grieved him to see his gentle pet tormented.

"Aw, fellows, don't tease him," he would protest.

"He's as much ours as he is yours," Dick would remind him. "Didn't we go partners in him?"

"Please, Tom, don't let them tease Pete," he would appeal to his oldest brother; but Tom always sided with Dick, so there would be noth-

ing left for him to do but to go off to his favorite spot on the front porch where he could
not see the bull fight and try to forget about
it by getting interested in some book. But
eventually Mr. Randall noticed how cross Pete
was becoming.

" There's no use in talking," he said to his
wife, " we'll just have to get rid of that lamb
of Eddie's. He's getting to be a regular
neighborhood nuisance."

" But Eddie is so fond of him," Mrs. Randall protested.

" Some day he'll hurt some one, you'll see,"
Mr. Randall prophesied, and there the matter
rested.

One day soon after this Mr. Obadiah H.
McCabe came into town to see Mr. Randall
about some law business. He was an eccentric
old bachelor, short, smooth-shaven, bald-
headed and stout, who when he came to town
always wore an old frock coat and a silk hat
that antedated the coat. He held mortgages
on about half the county and was very close-
fisted in money matters. This resulted in his
constantly being in lawsuits and made him one
of Mr. Randall's best clients. Yet with all his
peculiarities and his abnormal love of money

he had a warm spot in his heart for the Randall family and seldom came in from his farm without bringing some sort of gift either to Mrs. Randall or to one of the three boys.

On this occasion after his business with Mr. Randall had been completed he informed him:

"I've a dozen new-laid eggs here in this basket which I thought your wife might like."

"She'll be delighted to get them," said Mr. Randall cordially. "Why don't you take them up to the house yourself and have a little visit with her? I know she will be glad to have you. I'll finish up what I am doing here and will come along home in about half an hour and by then it will be dinner-time and you can stay and have dinner with us."

Pleased with the prospect of getting a dinner for nothing and of having a visit with Mrs. Randall, the little old gentleman trotted off up the street carrying his basket of eggs. As he entered the Randall gate Pete was occupying his favorite spot on the front door-mat. He looked with some disfavor on the squat little figure in the high hat approaching to disturb him and sniffed suspiciously at the basket.

At that Pete might have gotten up and let

the visitor pass unchallenged but for an unfortunate incident. The day was warm and Obadiah H. McCabe was portly and had been walking fast. As he reached the top step he set down the basket of eggs and drew forth a large red bandana handkerchief with the intention of wiping the perspiration from his brow before making his presence known.

The red bandana waved before him to Pete's mind could mean nothing but a challenge. He hastily scrambled to his feet and with an angry bleat charged at the unsuspecting old gentleman. The impact of Pete's hard head against his legs took Mr. McCabe entirely by surprise. He stumbled against the basket of eggs, knocking them down the steps, and then toppled over backwards right into the mess they made. His silk hat, too, rolled off and went bumping down the steps. Pete, for a moment bewildered by the outcome of his attack, stood there eying the havoc he had made and then charged after the hat. He soon succeeded in reducing it to utter ruin and in some way managed to get it entangled in his growing horns. Unable to shake it loose he turned in search of some new foe.

Mr. McCabe, his body badly bruised, and his self-esteem in a much worse condition, had just succeeded in collecting his scattered wits enough to try to get up and had managed to painfully raise himself on all fours. Once more Pete valiantly charged from behind and butted him over to earth again.

Just at this minute, Black Maggie, attracted by the commotion, came to the front door to see what was the matter. The sight she beheld was too much for her sense of humor. She burst into shrieks of laughter that quickly brought Mrs. Randall to the scene.

Mrs. Randall knew she should not have laughed, but who could have helped doing so? There on the ground was poor little fat bald Mr. McCabe, hatless, with his frock coat all yellow with egg, trying to get to his feet. There right beside him was the bellicose Pete, looking thoroughly ridiculous with the battered silk hat on his horns, butting over Mr. McCabe every time he tried to get up, both of them getting angrier and angrier every time it happened.

Mrs. Randall and Black Maggie both held their sides and laughed and laughed and laughed.

Sputtering with wrath Mr. McCabe at last managed to get to his feet. He aimed a vicious

but futile kick at Pete and with one furious
glance at his audience, strode hatless down the
street, endeavoring as far as was possible in
his disheveled condition to assume an air of
injured hauteur.

Mr. Randall, just leaving his office, caught
a glimpse of Mr. McCabe climbing into his
buggy at the livery-stable. He ran after him
and called out to ask what was the matter.
The only answer he received was a fist shaken
angrily at him as the hatless occupant of the
buggy drove rapidly in the direction of home.

With a feeling of disaster impending, Mr.
Randall hurried to his own house to find out
what had happened. Even he could not help
laughing as his wife described his client's encounter with Pete.

"It will be no laughing matter for us,
though," he announced, "for old Mr. McCabe
has been one of my best clients and probably
he never will speak to me again. One thing
is settled. Those boys have got to get rid of
that animal this very day before he does any
more damage."

"I suppose so," said Mrs. Randall, "but I
know it is going to break Eddie's heart to part
with his pet."

"I can't help that. Let Tom and Richard take him away this afternoon while Eddie is making his daily call on old Jonas. I don't care what they do with Pete. They can sell him or give him away. I don't want to find him here when I come home this evening."

So when Eddie came home late that afternoon Pete was missing.

"Where's my lamb?" he inquired anxiously.

"We sold him," Tom announced.

"What," cried Eddie, hardly believing his ears, "sold my lamb!"

"Yep," said Dick, "he butted old Mr. Obadiah H. McCabe down our front steps to-day and Dad ordered us to get rid of him right away. The butcher gave us six dollars for him."

"And here's the eighty-nine cents you put in," said Tom, handing him the money.

Mechanically Eddie took it, for a moment too stunned to think about anything except that his pet was gone. He was beginning to be somewhat of a philosopher and he comforted himself in the thought that anyhow Pete since he had grown so big and cross was not nearly so satisfactory a playmate as he had been at first. He felt, too, that Dad's order was a just one. By and by, too, his sense of arithmetic began to clamor for recognition.

" How much did you say you got for Pete," he demanded.

" Six dollars," Dick blurted out again, unmindful of a warning glance from Tom.

Eddie slowly counted over the money in his hand.

" Say," he protested, " we all three were partners and if you got six dollars —"

" What's the matter," said Dick," didn't we give you back all the money you put into it and you had all the fun of taking care of him besides —"

" Yes, but I put in most of the money and I ought —"

" Hold on," interrupted Tom, " it was our scheme, wasn't it? And we let you come in on it and we let you have the lamb to play with, didn't we? "

" Yes, but —"

" Eighty-nine cents is right," insisted Dick firmly.

" Yep," agreed Tom. " It's right."

With his two brothers against him Eddie felt it was useless to protest further, but the next afternoon he related his grievances in full to old Jonas.

"And while I was away," he said in conclusion, "they took Pete to the butcher and sold him and got six dollars — six whole dollars for him and all he cost was a dollar and a quarter. I'd put in eighty-nine cents of it but all they gave me back out of the six dollars was my own eighty-nine cents. Do you think that was fair?"

"Yes and no," said old Jonas after a moment's meditation while he refilled his pipe. "You see you oughtn't to have gone partners with them without having everything understood. Before you put your money in you should have asked who was to take care of the lamb and how much you were to get if the lamb was sold for a profit. All you was looking for when you went into the partnership was a little woolly lamb to play with and that's what you got. Tom and Richard was looking for something else and they got it, too. Ain't that right, Eddie?"

"Yes," said the little lame boy thoughtfully, "I guess you are right. I wasn't thinking about money when I went partners. I was only thinking about the lamb."

" And your brothers, I'll warrant," said old Jonas, " were thinking most about the money, and in this world people generally get what they think most about. And remember this, Eddie, partners is partners even when they're your own brothers."

CHAPTER TEN

"I'M NOT A 'FRAID-CAT!"

"MR. JONAS," said Eddie, looking up into the face of the grizzled one-legged veteran, who sat sunning himself in front of his tobacco-shop, "are you ever afraid of anything?"

Jonas Tucker looked quizzically down at Edward Haverford Randall, perched on the top of an upturned box, and meditated a moment before making his reply.

"Yes and no," he said at length. "You see, it's this way: I used to be scared of a lot of things, but somehow as I get older, there don't seem to be many things left worth being scared of."

"Well, when you were afraid, what were you afraid of?" demanded the boy.

"Well, let's see," said Jonas, "after I had my leg off, I used to be scared I mightn't be able to earn a living and might have to die in the poorhouse. There was years and years that I worried about that, and what good did it do me? Here I am, well over seventy, and have never been near the poorhouse yet. Even if I had to go now, I don't think I'd be afraid of it. I'd have a roof over my head and a place to sleep, and I don't eat much anyhow; so what difference would it make?"

"No, I s'pose it wouldn't, and I could come and see you there, too, couldn't I?"

"You bet you could," replied Jonas warmly. "I just wouldn't stay anywhere where they wouldn't let you come. So, you see, Eddie, it don't pay to be afraid of things. Most of the things we're afraid of never hurt us."

"Were you ever afraid of cows?" asked Eddie irrelevantly.

Old Jonas nodded sagely. "So that's it, is it?"

"Yes," said Eddie miserably, "that's it. I was going along the street with Tom and Richard, and a cow came along, and I ducked, and they laughed and called me 'fraid-cat."

"I'll warrant they did. And are you afraid of cows?"

"Yes," admitted Eddie truthfully, "I guess I am; at least, I'm scared of cows I'm not acquainted with."

"For all that," said old Jonas, "I don't know as that makes you a 'fraid-cat even if your brothers did call you one. You see, Eddie, they don't understand. A fellow with two good legs always figures that if anything comes after him, he can run and get away. Now, a fellow with only a leg and a half has always got to look where he's going. I wouldn't call him a 'fraid-cat for doing that; he's just being sensible and cautious."

"But I don't like being called 'fraid-cat," protested the youngster, a little in doubt as to Jonas's philosophy.

"That's no way to look at it. If you are a 'fraid-cat, people have a right to call you one. If you're not, and you know you're not, why it doesn't make any difference what they call you."

"I guess I understand," said Eddie thoughtfully, "and I'm going to try never to be a 'fraid-cat. Tom and Dick can say it all they want to, but I'll try not to mind a bit."

"That's the ticket!" said old Jonas. "Nobody could do more'n that — not even a two-legged fellow."

That evening Mr. and Mrs. Randall were discussing the very same subject. What brought it up was a letter from Mrs. Randall's Aunt Carrie Mason. She and her husband lived in a little farm village about twenty miles away.

"I wish," said her letter, "you would let one of the boys come and make us a week's visit. Any one of the three will do. You surely can spare one of them that long."

"Better send Eddie," suggested Mr. Randall. "I heard Tom and Richard calling him a 'fraid-cat because he ran from a cow. Better send him out among the cows and make a man of him. It will do him a lot of good. You baby him too much."

"Poor little fellow," said Mrs. Randall, utterly unconscious of her husband's last remark. "Yes, I think we would better let Eddie go. He has so few amusements."

So it was settled that Eddie should go to Aunt Carrie's.

"A farm's no place for a 'fraid-cat," said Dick scornfully. "You better watch out or the cows'll eat you."

"I don't see why they let you go," said Tom. "A farm is a great place for hunting, and you can't hunt."

But Eddie, mindful of Jonas's good advice,

only smiled happily. He did not care if Dick did call him a 'fraid-cat. He had made up his mind not to let himself be afraid of anything ever again. So long as he knew he wasn't a 'fraid-cat, what difference did it make?

His first day on the farm was one wonderful round of excitement. All day long he was about the place with Uncle John or Aunt Carrie, taking personal interest in and asking many questions about everything he saw.

"Don't you keep any cows, Uncle John?" he inquired politely, not without a quaver in his voice. If they did have cows, he wondered how he was going to keep from being afraid of them. He had already thoroughly inspected the barn, the pig-pens, and the dog-house. Nowhere could he see any evidence of the presence of cattle, although he had always supposed that everybody in the country kept cows of their own.

"No," said Uncle John, "we haven't had any cows for years. You see, there are only the two of us, and it would hardly be worth while. We get what milk we need at Henry Young's place across the fields there. You can go with me for the milk after supper if you want to."

Of course he wanted to, and after the evening meal he and Uncle John took a pail and set out across the fields. It was rather a long walk for Eddie, nearly a quarter of a mile, but there were so many interesting novelties about the journey that he hardly noticed the distance. There were the bars to the pasture and a stile with steps, and a gate to which was attached a bucket of stones on a chain so that it closed itself, all of which were new to him.

The prospect of meeting people also appealed to the little lame chap. Hitherto his acquaintances had been limited to a few people in the town in which he lived, the boys and girls he knew at school, the families that went to the same church. He thoroughly enjoyed being introduced to Farmer Young and his wife, to their daughter, and to the two hired men, Joe and Sam. He was interested in seeing the great stables with rows of stalls, one for each cow, and in watching the farmer's daughter and the two men milking and carrying the great pails of foaming milk to the dairy to be strained and emptied into huge cans. The old-fashioned spring-house with its crocks of cream set in the cold water, the churns, the buttermilk barrel, everything was so interesting and novel that Eddie was sorry when Uncle John, through chatting with Farmer Young, was ready to depart.

When they got back home, Eddie, tired from traveling, from the excitement, from the trip after the milk, was quite ready to go to bed. It was a pleasant novelty to go up-stairs with a candle instead of turning on the electric light as they did at home. His aunt conducted him to a small room in the attic where he was to sleep. After he had undressed and got into bed, he hesitated just a minute as he started to blow out his candle.

All of a sudden a great sense of loneliness — of homesickness — came over him. He remembered that it was the first time in his life that he had gone to bed without a good-night kiss from his mother. Up to this time he had been so busy and so interested that he had not even thought about her. He wondered if she was missing him. He wondered what his brothers and dad were doing. He wondered if they were thinking about him. He wished he could see them all. He was almost sorry he had come.

Fear began to creep over him — terror of the dark, terror of the unknown. He dared not blow out the candle and leave himself all alone there in the darkness. He was so far away from every one, up there in the attic. His imagination began to picture all sorts of terrible things that might happen to him. He wanted his mother so, or Tom, or Richard, or Jonas —

At the thought of old Jonas, his parting words of advice came back to Eddie. He wasn't a 'fraid-cat! He wouldn't be a 'fraid-cat! There wasn't anything to fear. Resolutely he raised himself under the covers and blew out the candle, sinking back in bed with a little shiver.

The next thing he knew he heard Aunt Carrie's voice at the foot of the stairs bidding him hurry or he would be late to breakfast.

Very pleasantly indeed passed the second day of his visit, and before he realized it, it was supper-time again.

"I've got to go down to the post-office this evening," said Uncle John, as he got up from the table. "Eddie, I wonder if you could go for the milk alone tonight. You know the way."

"Sure I could!" cried the boy delightedly. "May I?" It made him feel very important and useful to be called on to do some one a service.

"I'm afraid it's too much of a walk for him with his lameness," objected Aunt Carrie, "and I wanted ten cents' worth of cream as well as the milk tonight. I was going to make a shortcake tomorrow. I'm afraid Eddie can't manage two pails."

"A shortcake," shouted Eddie, "you bet I can carry both pails! That's nothing, I often carry things."

So with a pail in each hand he hobbled off across the fields. Some way the trip this time seemed far longer than it had when he was with his uncle. He was so long in arriving at the gate that he was beginning to be afraid that he had missed his way, and it was not until he was in sight of the Youngs' farmhouse that he was quite certain about it. When he arrived, he was decidedly glad that he had come. So many interesting things had happened since he had been there the evening before. Joe had shot a hawk that had been after the chickens and had kept the dead bird to show to Eddie. There was a weasel, too, that had been trapped as it tried to steal eggs. Sam had skinned it and after rubbing salt in the skin had tacked it on the barn-door to dry.

"My!" said Eddie, as he examined it and felt the soft fur, " I wish Brother Tom was here to see that."

There was a new little calf in the barn, which Eddie inspected with wondering admiration, and he had to hear how the bees had swarmed, which accounted for their being late with the milking that evening. Altogether there was so much to see and so many questions to ask that he almost forgot what he had come for.

" It's getting dark," Mrs. Young called out. " Eddie, you'd better be getting home with that milk."

Getting dark! It was dark. By the time Eddie had loaded up with his pail of milk and his smaller pail of cream and was ready to set out for home, he could not see any distance in front of him. With quaking heart he plunged forth into the unknown. The gate, easy enough to get through in the daytime, loomed up as the first difficulty. He had to set one of the pails down, carry the other through, and then come back and get the second pail.

He shivered with nervous dread as he hobbled on across the field. The thousand and one strange noises of the night terrified him. He wanted to hurry, to run, but he found that he could not. Whenever he sought to quicken his pace, he found that both the milk and the cream would slop out of the pails. The only way he could manage to carry them safely was to walk very slowly and carefully, for his gait at the best was irregular. Each step he took seemed to be carrying him farther and farther into a land of unknown terrors. As he left the lights of the farmhouse behind him, a terrible sense of desolation and loneliness overtook him. Trees, bushes, and little clumps of grass in the darkness assumed all sorts of unfamiliar and soul-shaking shapes.

As he peered ahead of him, trying to see the path, he stopped short with a shudder. He saw something moving, something coming toward him. Nearer and nearer came the indistinct, grotesque figure. He wanted to scream. His throat seemed to close. His heart began to pump wildly. His knees shook. He heard something go " sniff, sniff."

Visions of all kinds of fierce wild beasts passed through his head. Maybe it was a bear. He turned to flee, but stumbled and fell.

Both pails went crashing down with a great clatter. From the darkness came a startled "wumpf." The terrifying shape seemed to rise in the air and vanished.

For a moment Eddie lay where he had fallen, great sobs of fright wracking his slender body. "I'm not a 'fraid-cat," he kept resolutely saying to himself. "I'm not! I'm not! I won't be!"

At last he managed to get to his feet. He was horrified to find that the contents of both pails had been spilled. What was to be done about it? Maybe Uncle John and Aunt Carrie would be angry with him. It was the first errand with which they had trusted him. There was no way out of it. He must go back through the terrifying darkness and get some more milk and cream. In his pocket was a quarter, a bright new quarter, that dad had given him for spending money. He would go back and give it to Mrs. Young and tell her he had spilled the milk and cream and ask her for some more. He hoped that he would have enough money to pay for it. He would not tell Uncle John and Aunt Carrie anything about it. If he did, they would never trust him again. Maybe Joe or Sam would walk back with him across the fields this time. No, he decided, he wasn't a 'fraid-cat. He would not let them come with him even if they wanted to. He would get the pails refilled and would carry them home all by himself. He would not let any one imagine that he was afraid. He just would say that he had tripped and spilled the milk and cream and would ask for some more.

Resolutely he made his way back to the dairy. Mrs. Young quickly refilled the pails and would not take his money.

"Accidents will happen," she said cheerily, "and watch out you don't stumble this time."

If it took courage to set out for home the first time, it took still greater valor to start the second time. The first time Eddie had feared there might be unknown dangers in the dark. This time he knew! Somewhere in the field beyond the gate a great wild beast of some sort lay in wait for him. He had seen it dimly through the darkness. He had heard it sniffing at him. If the noise of the falling pails had not scared it off, there was no telling what might have happened to him. He looked about for a stick or club but could find none.

Even if he had a weapon, he could not carry it, as his hands were full.

The night seemed to be getting blacker and blacker. Up in the sky were thousands and thousands of stars, but they did not seem to give any light at all. Vaguely Eddie wondered why they did not have street-lamps in the country. He had been out at night lots and lots of times at home, but there were always lights enough there to see where you were going. Here there were no lights at all.

He could barely make out the path by which he had come. Still badly shaken by his previous experience, he now began to seem to see things moving all about him. The cold sweat gathered on his forehead. Strange rustlings and squeakings came from all sides. Sometimes his foot descending fell on a clump of grass instead of the path, and it was as if he had walked on something alive. He would start and shudder and hesitate, hardly daring to take another step, yet he forced himself to go on and on.

At last he reached the gate again. What lay in wait for him behind it? Was the mysterious animal still there? Carefully he set down the pail of cream and, holding the gate open, got the milk safely through. He returned for the cream. So far nothing had happened, but it was living torture to go through the gate once more carrying the cream, plunging again into the horrors of the unknown.

Step by step he felt his way through the darkness, growing more and more terrified as he approached the spot where he had encountered the animal. He strained his eyes in vain trying to see what lay before him. Shaking in every limb he advanced carefully, cautiously, debating what he should do in case he was confronted by — he knew not what. He hardly dared breathe.

Terror of a new sort seized him. He wondered if he was on the right path. He stopped stock-still and tried to ascertain where he was. A little off to the right was something, a vague black shape, that looked like a tree. He did not recall having seen it when he made the trip in the daylight. Where was he? Oh, if mother was only there with him, or dad, they would know what to do, which way to go.

But he wasn't afraid! He mustn't be afraid. Under his breath he whispered,

" Now I lay me," and " Our Father," fearful of saying the words out loud lest he might attract the attention of some wandering night beast or goblin. Once more, drawing a long breath, he resolutely set forth, dragging along step by step, fearful of going forward, terrified to go back, more scared still to remain where he was.

Suddenly, right beside him, almost in the path, some great animal arose and whirled to face him. He could see two great eyes glaring at him. It was so close that even in the darkness he could see it move. He could hear again that terrifying " sniff, sniff," he could almost feel its breath in his face.

He stopped stock-still in sheer terror, his hands trembling so that he could hardly hold the pails. Through his fear-stricken brain just one thought kept running over and over again. " I'm not a 'fraid-cat! I'm not! I'm not! "

Step by step he advanced toward the beast that stood facing him. Closer and closer he came to it until it seemed that if he took another step he would come up against it. With a grunt it wheeled and again seemed to rise in the air, then sped away in the darkness.

Somewhat relieved by its disappearance, but still in the grip of terror, Eddie hobbled on and on. As he was climbing over the stile, he saw a light come bobbing across the fields. New terror smote him. The fantastic motions of the wavering light as it came nearer and nearer filled him with strange dread. What was it? Who was it? Perhaps it was a robber. He recalled with growing terror that the stile was hardly more than half-way to his uncle's house. He still had a long journey through the darkness ahead of him. Once more he set out valiantly, carefully carrying both pails, watching with growing apprehension the fantastic bobbing of the light as it came nearer and nearer.

"Is that you, Eddie?" came his uncle's voice out of the darkness.

Never before had he heard such a welcome sound. A wave of relief, a feeling that all peril was past, swept over him. For a moment he was too overcome to speak.

"Yes, it's me," he managed to whisper at last.

"Thought you was lost," said Uncle John as he emerged from the darkness, carrying a lantern.

"No," explained the boy, still trembling from his fright, "I fell and spilled the milk and had to go back and get some more."

"That was it, was it?" said his uncle. "I thought maybe that bull calf in the next pasture had eaten you up."

"Was that only a bull calf?" exclaimed Eddie in surprise.

"Sure, what did you think it was?"

"I didn't know," Eddie confessed as he clutched one of his uncle's hands, "but I was awfully scared of it."

"Pooh," said his uncle, "you need never be scared of a calf. They are just playful. None of the cows round here are cross."

"I'm glad of that," said the boy.

A week later Eddie, safe home again, was recounting his adventures to his brothers: "And over at the farm where we went for the milk, Joe — he's one of the hired men, shot a great big hawk, and the same day they trapped a weasel, and Sam — he's the other hired man — he skinned it and tacked the skin up on the barn-door, and that same day the bees swarmed. And that evening I stayed so long that it was pitch-dark when I went to go home, and I had to walk all by myself through three great big fields, and a great big bull calf was right there in the path —"

"What did you do?" asked Tom.

"I'll bet you was scared to death," said Dick.

Vivid as are the terrors of childhood, the impression they make is not a lasting one, and, besides, it is not boy-nature to admit short-comings to other boys. With never a blush, Eddie continued his narrative almost boast-fully: "Pooh, I'm no 'fraid-cat. I just walked right up to it, and it turned and ran away."

CHAPTER ELEVEN

"MR. JONAS," questioned Eddie, "do you like ice-cream?"

"Yes and no," replied the old man thoughtfully. He knew that the boy was expecting an answer in the affirmative. No boy of ten can understand how any one could possibly *not* like ice-cream. Jonas was hesitating how to find an answer that would not hurt his little friend's sensitive feelings. "I can't deny I like the taste of it right well but, you see, Eddie, the coldness of it hurts my teeth something dreadful."

As he answered he was studying Eddie's face, to see the effect of his reply. Life with one leg had made him understand how often youngsters like Eddie, maimed or deformed in any way, are apt to be morbid and over-sensitive. Not for the world would he have done or said anything to offend the one person in the world who thought enough of him to come to see him every day. The companionship of the boy and the trust Eddie put in all his judgments were far too precious a possession to be endangered by any careless rejection of some proffered gift.   From past experience he knew that Eddie liked to share with him whatever brought him pleasure.

"I like ice-cream," announced Eddie, "and it doesn't hurt my teeth a bit.   If I eat it too fast though it gives me a funny pain right across my nose."

"Yes," said Jonas, nodding sagaciously, "it's apt to do just that."

"What I was going to say," Eddie continued, "was that we are going to have ice-cream for our Sunday dinner and I'll get mother to let me bring you some if you'd like it."

The old man, sitting before his little tobacco shop, brushed a suspicious moisture from his eyes and made pretense of lighting his pipe. When you are well past seventy and poor and crippled few persons — very few indeed — remember to do kindly acts for you.   The youngster's thoughtfulness for him touched him deeply.

"Well now, it's mighty nice of you, Eddie, to think of me when you have ice-cream," he

exclaimed warmly, " but I'll have to take the
will for the deed. I'd like the ice-cream all
right but my teeth would ache afterward and
it isn't worth it."

" No, I s'pose it isn't."

" You see, Eddie, when you get as old as me
you begin to figure on consequences. It's different with boys. They go ahead and do
everything and eat everything and never
think about what's going to happen afterward."

" I guess that's right. Tom and Richard
and I out in Mr. S. T. Adams's orchard one
day ate a lot of green apples and we had awful
pains afterward."

" I'll warrant you did," chuckled old Jonas.
" That's just the trouble with all boys —
they're so frog-minded."

" I didn't know frogs had any minds," said
Eddie, looking puzzled.

" I don't suppose they have," explained
Jonas, " but that wasn't what I meant. Boys
are always jumping at things just like frogs,
and never looking where it'll land them."

" I never jump," protested Eddie plaintively. " I wish I could."

" Of course not," assented the veteran, " a

leg and a half ain't much for jumping with, but I didn't mean it that way. I meant jumping with your mind. I expect you're just as frog-minded as most other boys."

" But how can your mind jump? "

" It's this way — you see some green apples and your mind jumps and says, ' Let's eat them.' If you didn't let your mind jump it would be pretty sure to say, ' Hold on here, green apples will give me a stomach ache,' and then you wouldn't eat them."

" I guess that's right."

" You bet it is. It's being frog-minded that gets boys into most of their troubles. If they'd only stop to think instead of letting their minds jump they'd be far better off."

" But," asked Eddie, "how am I going to keep my mind from jumping? "

" Tain't so easy for a boy, nor for a man either," said Jonas. " There's only one way I know of."

" What's that? "

" Whenever you think about doing anything, think twice."

" Why that's just like doing arithmetic," said Eddie. " It sounds easy. I'm going to try it."

"Good!" said Jonas. "Thinking twice never did any one any harm, but I'll warrant you find it harder than doing your arithmetic."

Eddie departed filled with resolves never again to let himself be frog-minded and for a day or two he got quite a lot of amusement out of trying to keep his mind from jumping and from thinking twice about everything he set out to do. He found the plan worked fairly well. He was up in his room with the treasures from his chest scattered all over the floor. Tom called to him to come out to the barn. He started to run right out, but thinking twice about it, he stopped to tidy up his room before answering his brother's call. When he came in tired that evening he was glad the place was in order, for it was one of the inflexible rules of the house that each boy must put away all his playthings before going to bed.

Another time Maggie, the cook, asked him to go on an errand right when he was in the middle of an exciting chapter of a new book from the library. "Let Dick do it," he started to say, but thinking twice about it, he closed his book promptly and went cheerfully on Maggie's errand. After all she did so many kind

things for him that he felt it was his duty to
help her all he could.   At any rate the handful
of cookies she gave him on his return was ample
reward.

He began to take self-conscious pride in his
success in keeping his mind from jumping.
He decided that his new scheme of life was
making him a vastly better boy. He even confided to his mother as she came up-stairs to kiss
him good-night that he never again was going
to be frog-minded.

"What on earth are you talking about?"
she asked, puzzled by the phrase, but he vol-
unteered no further explanation, though he
gave himself a mental pat on the back as he
went asleep, feeling that he deserved great
credit for the success with which he was carrying out his plan.

But alas, for Eddie's good resolves. As
with most of us the unexpected occurrence all
too frequently upsets our intentions to reform
before they have had time to crystallize into
persistent and continuing habits. Jarred by
the unusual, we act on the spur of the moment,
without taking time to think twice about it,
and later we discover regretfully that we have
been guilty of doing the very thing that we so

firmly had determined we never were going to do again.

There came a Saturday morning — a morning with nothing especial to do — the kind of a morning that nearly always drives energetic boys into some sort of mischief. Bob Tucker and Four-eyed Smith came racing by the house as the three Randall boys idled on the front porch.

"Come on, fellers," cried Bob excitedly, "come on along and see it."

"Come on, come on," panted Four-eyed Smith, striving vainly to run as fast as the Tucker boy.

"Where are you going?" asked Tom.

"What is it? What's going on?" asked Dick, already scrambling to his feet.

"Come along and see," cried the vanishing Bob. "I can't stop to tell you."

Tom, too, was on his feet by now and even Eddie, putting aside the book he was reading, began awkwardly to get to his feet, wondering what it was that had excited the boys so.

"It's a railroad wreck, a terrible wreck — down back of the station," called Four-eyed over his shoulder.

Before the words were fairly out of his

mouth Tom and Richard were at his heels, and, newer in the race and less short of breath, quickly were outdistancing him.

A thrill came to Eddie, too, at the wonderful opportunity. A railroad wreck! He had read of wrecks but never had he seen one. Never before so far as he knew had there ever been one in the vicinity. He just must see what it looked like. He might never have another opportunity of seeing a wreck. His vivid imagination began picturing the two locomotives coming together with whistles blowing and bells ringing. It must be a grand sight.

He started to run after the others — no, he didn't run. He couldn't. For him to run with his weak leg and its heavy brace was a perilous impossibility. He tried it for a few futile steps and then settled down to the fastest gait that was possible for him, a method of progress that may best be described as a hasty hobble.

As he limped breathlessly after the others he was still continuing to picture to himself the horrors of a wreck. He was wondering how it would look to see a row of passenger-cars all upside down and smashed, with some of them burning. He could see in his imagination the passengers scrambling out of the cars. He could hear their shrieks. Some of them might be lying there dead or senseless. It must be a wonderful sight to see and maybe there would be an opportunity for him to help rescue somebody or to bind up a wound and save some lady's life.

Then the distressing thought came that it might be all over before he got there. Tom and Richard and the other boys would get there in time to see everything and he might be too late.

" Wait — wait for me! " he shrieked after his vanishing brothers. " Wait for me! "

They gave no indication that they had heard him, but kept on running until they were out of sight.

" Please wait for me! " he called again with a plaintive sob in his throat. Several times he had to stop to get his breath and to check the sharp little pain that came in his side. Yet despairingly he kept on, his active mind busy with many things but never once recalling what was Dad's firmest injunction:

" Never go near the railroad tracks! "

Time and time again Mr. Randall had

warned all three of the boys of the perils of playing about the railroad. In winter-time some of the boys when they were making sleds were in the habit of pilfering from box cars the wooden bars used when the doors are open. Such pieces of seasoned oak stood high in favor for making sled runners. Mr. Randall had sternly denounced this practise as nothing less than stealing and had even gone so far as to forbid Tom and Richard from riding on Froggie Sweeney's sled built of railroad material.

"But," Tom had asked at the time, "there's nothing wrong, is there, in walking the rails when there are no trains coming? All the fellows do it."

One of the favorite competitive amusements of the boys of the town was to see how many rails they could walk without once stepping off.

"Lots of boys have been killed and injured doing that very thing," said Mr. Randall. "I forbid all you boys ever doing it. I want you to stay away from the railroad tracks altogether."

"Can't we even make scissors?" asked Dick. "You don't have to go on the tracks at all to do that. You just lay your pins on the track and wait until after the train has passed over them."

" No," said Mr. Randall, " you must not do that either. I want each of you to promise me that you will never play on or near the tracks. Promise me, Tom."

" I promise," said Tom.

" I promise," said Richard.

Eddie felt at the time that the lecture had not been aimed at him for he never even had wanted to play on the tracks, still, just to be on a par with the others, he, too, had said:

" I promise."

This injunction of their father's was a sore point with Tom and Richard. Nearly all the other boys of their acquaintance had escaped without any such orders. The other fellows had all sorts of coins flattened by trains passing over them and pins mashed flat into funny-looking little daggers and crossed pins pressed into " scissors." Froggie Sweeney even had a pair of " scissors " made from two horse-shoe nails.

But none of all this came into Eddie's mind at the moment. He was obsessed with the desire of seeing a railroad wreck. The only thing that was worrying him was that it might be all over before he got there.

He felt somewhat relieved as he came within sight of the tracks to observe a crowd standing there. There must still be something to see. He tried to hurry as he started to cross the tracks of the freight yard and stumbling on a rail fell full length, scratching his hands on the ballast and tearing his trousers across the knee. A man who was passing called out to know if he was hurt.

"No sir," he answered as he scrambled to his feet. "I'm not hurt. I'm used to falling."

In his eagerness to reach the scene of the accident he hardly realized that his hands were cut and bleeding. When at last he had wormed his way through the crowd and reached the front row where the other boys had long since arrived his first sensation was one of great disappointment. There was nothing much to see after all.

It had been only a freight wreck. One box car with its end smashed and one of its trucks twisted around lay on its side near where it had been derailed. The locomotive that had done the damage had disappeared. No one, apparently, had been killed or injured. All

there was to be seen was a gang of laborers re-
pairing the track where the collision had taken
place. Quickly the men who had been attracted to the scene began to withdraw. Soon
only a group of boys was left and for perhaps
half an hour they stood around waiting for
something more to happen. At last it happened. The yard-master, up to his neck in
work as a result of the mishap, came by.

" What are you youngsters doing here? " he
called out in angry tones. " Get out of here,
every one of you! "

Sullenly but hastily the boys, recognizing his
authority in the matter, split up into little
groups and started to leave. Eddie and his
brothers and the other two boys started across
the tracks in the direction of home.

" He's got his nerve chasing us out when we
weren't doing anything," commented Bob
Tucker resentfully.

" A wreck ain't such a much after all," said
Four-eyed Smith, voicing the disappointment
all of them had experienced at finding so little
to be excited about.

Tom was silent, gloomily hoping that his
father would not hear that they had disobeyed
his explicit orders. He was mentally trying

to excuse himself on the ground that a wreck made an exceptional case but his conscience would not be stilled by any such argument.

Just as they reached and crossed the last of the tracks in safety a long freight train came backing slowly down to pick up some cars.

" Gee, if we only had some pins it would be a dandy chance to make some scissors," suggested Dick.

" Wouldn't it? " assented Tom.

" But Dad has forbidden our doing it," remonstrated Eddie. All of a sudden his father's many injunctions about playing on the railroad tracks had popped into his mind. He was feeling very wretched and miserable and guilty about it. He wanted to get away from there and get home as fast as he could.

" Aw, shut up, Limpy," commanded Tom savagely, not caring to have his already troubled conscience stimulated by any such reminders from his youngest brother. " It would be no worse than what you've been doing. Who's got any pins? "

Eddie, hurt by his brother's gruffness, sensitive always about having either of his brothers speak of him as " Limpy," grew red and was silent.

" You're a nice one to be talking about us," added Richard. " You are in it just as deep as we are. What are you doing here any- how? "

Even at this added rebuke Eddie held his peace. What *was* he doing here? If only he had remembered to think twice — if he had not been so frog-minded — if he hadn't jumped and hurried to see the wreck, he would have recalled his promise. He felt so ashamed and so sorry. He had broken his promise to Dad. What right had he to reprove his brothers? He was equally guilty with them.

None of them had been able to find any pins. The train had stopped, coupled on the extra cars and had begun to move slowly out of the yard. To Tom, standing sullenly beside the track, came a new idea. He had arrived at the age when he felt he was too big to be bossed by his father. He resented Eddie's having reminded him before the other boys that he was not allowed to play on the tracks. He felt that he must do something, something new, something daring, to regain prestige in their eyes.

" Dare you to jump on the next car," he challenged Bob Tucker.

Bob looked rather dubiously at the passing train of freight cars. It was something he never had tried and he, too, had had his orders from home about playing on the tracks. But the code of boyhood forbade his taking a dare.

" I dare if you dare," he retorted.

" Come on then," cried the reckless Tom, who had not anticipated that his dare would be taken in earnest and now felt that it was up to him to make good.

Making a running leap, Tom managed to grasp the iron brace on the side of one of the cars and at the same time to get one foot on the iron step. Clinging there he turned halfway around to shout defiance at Bob Tucker.

" Oh, Tom, don't," shrieked Eddie, terrified at such temerity.

Tucker started running alongside of the train and managed to land on the step of the car behind Tom with equal success. Not to be outdone by Tom he clambered up on to the car platform and stood there holding on with one hand and waving the other at Tom.

Four-eyed Smith and Dick, envious of the daring of their leaders but not having courage enough to try to emulate them, began running alongside the train on the cinder path. Eddie stood silent, spellbound with terror.

The train began to gather speed. Dick, running as fast as he could beside it found that he was losing ground.

" You'd better jump off," he called out to Tom, " she's going like sixty."

Tom had already been trying to muster up his courage to get off. From where he clung the train seemed to be going at a terrific rate. He had begun to realize that getting off was going to be a far harder task than getting on had been. When he heard Dick's warning he let himself down as far as he dared and let go. The momentum of the train whirled him over but fortunately he fell away from the track and quickly scrambled to his feet unhurt.

As he fell he had a glimpse of Bob Tucker's white frightened face. He had been just about to jump off when he saw Tom's fall and it terrified him so that he let go of the car step while still holding on to the brace. For a second he clung there, swaying against the car, and then, unable to retain his hold any longer, slipped and fell right down on the ties, with one of his arms and one of his legs right under the car wheels.

There was one shrill scream of agonized pain and then a deathlike silence. Bob lay white and still, so close beside the rails that the passing cars all but grazed his head.

" Bob's killed! Bob's killed! "

It was Eddie's frantic shouts that finally attracted the attention of the flagman on the last car and of the laborers at work near by. Some one ran for a doctor. What happened afterward was all a daze so far as Eddie Randall was concerned. He recalled hearing a man's voice saying:

" He'll live — if you call it living with one hand and one leg gone."

Eddie must have fainted right after that. When, for days and nights afterward, he tried to think about it, he could not remember how he and Tom and Richard had gotten home. He did remember that his mother came running down the street to meet them, gathering them all in her arms and hugging and kissing them in turn. She had heard about the accident — somehow mothers always do hear it quickly when anything happens to a boy.

Eddie's shirt was all wet in front where some one had spilled water on him when he fainted. His hands, too, were all cut and bleeding where he had fallen on the tracks. At first his mother was fearful that he, too, had been injured. She began to weep hysterically.

" That's only water," Tom hastened to explain. " He fainted after it happened."

" But his hands —"

" He fell on the ballast and scratched himself."

She was not satisfied until she had them all safe in the house and had looked them over from head to foot. They were all strangely silent and oppressed, awed by the morning's tragedy. Finding them all unhurt she began to reproach them for having disobeyed their father, but her reproaches were cut short.

Eddie, overwrought by what he had witnessed, began to sob and to shriek hysterically:

" Oh, mother, mother, I'll never be frog-minded again. I'll never be frog-minded again."

Alarmed at his outburst, failing utterly to understand what he was talking about, she began to fear that the sight of the tragedy had been too much for his nerves and had perhaps affected his reason. Hurrying him up-stairs to bed she made him drink a glass of hot milk and sat with her arms around him comforting

him and soothing him until finally he fell
asleep.

When she came down-stairs again she found
the other two boys still sitting silent and depressed in the dining room where she had left
them.

" You boys both go up-stairs and go to bed
and stay there all day," she directed.   She felt
that they needed some sort of punishment, but
she was in no mood to inflict it.   She was too
thankful that they had all come back to her
safe and sound.   What if it had been one of
her darling boys who had lost a leg and an arm.
How sorry she felt, too, for Mrs. Tucker.   But
she must send Tom and Richard to bed.
Then, at last, she really felt they were safe.
The boys, to her amazement, made no protest
against her order, even though it was not yet
noon.   As a matter of fact they welcomed the
idea.   Anything was better just at present
than having to face father when he came home
to lunch.   At the stairs she stopped them for
a moment.

" Do either of you boys know what Eddie
meant by being frog-minded? "

" No," said Tom.   " I've no idea what he
meant."

" He never said it to me," added Dick.

She was still puzzling about Eddie's curious phrase when Mr. Randall came home.

" Please don't punish the boys or say anything to them about it," she urged him as they discussed the morning's direful happenings. " They were all very disobedient, I know, but I think they have been punished enough. Eddie was all worked up about it and I have sent them all to bed for the day."

" I guess they've all had a lesson," said Mr. Randall; " a lesson they'll never forget."

" I'm sure they won't," said Mrs. Randall, " but I wish I knew what Eddie meant."

" Why, what did he say? "

" He kept saying over and over again that he wasn't going to be frog-minded any more."

" That's a funny phrase," said her husband. " Probably it meant something about that Sweeney boy. They call him Froggie, don't they? "

" No," said Mrs. Randall, " I'm sure it wasn't that. Froggie Sweeney wasn't with them to-day. It had something to do with his going on the railroad tracks after you had forbade him. I wish I knew."

But to this day she never has found out.

Only old Jonas knows.   To him the next afternoon Eddie reaffirmed his pledge of his firm
intention never to be frog-minded again.

"I'll warrant you won't," said old Jonas,
adding sagely: "Sometimes the other fellow's licking learns us a lot."

CHAPTER TWELVE

A HOUSE AND A HOME

SOMETHING unusual and mysterious was happening in the Randall home. All three boys sensed it without being able to find out what it was. For a whole week dad and mother had been talking together in whispered conversations that ceased abruptly whenever one of their sons approached. Dad had gone about the house with his brows wrinkled in thought. Mrs. Randall seemed always to have a preoccupied air somewhat tinctured with sadness.

Whenever Tom or Richard or even Eddie started to ask dad questions, mother would always interrupt with: "Run away, boys, and don't bother father. He has something on his mind."

It was an entirely novel situation that confronted the youngsters. Hitherto dad had been to them, most of the time at least, a sort of extra playmate. Sometimes, it is true, he brought home papers with him from his law office.   On such occasions it was a well-understood rule of the household that he was not to be interrupted nor bothered.   But such occasions were rare and never lasted longer than one or two evenings.   At such times most of the punishments were ordered by mother, dad being called upon only in extreme cases, and as it happened all three boys for several days had been on their good behavior — or at least had not been detected in any unusual mischief. Yet somehow the conduct of both their parents gave them a premonition that something out of the ordinary was about to happen.

"It isn't a case," announced Dick positively. "Dad hasn't brought any papers home, and besides court doesn't meet till next month."

"It's nothing we've done," asserted Tom reflectively.   "Whenever dad finds anything out, he gets right after us and has it over with."

"No," agreed Dick.   "He's got nothing on us."

"Maybe," suggested Eddie, feeling very important and honored at being admitted into the counsels of his elders, "maybe, Tom, he's trying to make up his mind to let you get a job."

"Naw," said Tom gloomily, "you're wrong

there, Limpy. He'd as soon let you go to work as he would me. I've talked to him dozens of times, and he only laughs at me."

The red of shame crept into Eddie's cheeks as Tom in his preoccupation called him by the hated epithet. He resented, too, his oldest brother's taking it for granted that he never would be able to work. Down in his heart he was confident that he could handle a job just as well as Tom could, and some day he was going to show them all. Yet so sensitive was he about his lameness that even to his own brothers he never made any retort when they reminded him of it.

" Tell you what," suggested Dick, " I'll bet he's figuring if he can afford to send Eddie to New York to get his leg fixed. I heard him and mother talking about it once. Dad said it would cost more than he could afford."

" Naw," said Tom decisively, " that's not it. They gave up that idea long ago."

Once more Eddie colored up. He did wish people would not talk about his lameness in front of him. Mortified by the repeated references to " it "— the hideous, ever-present " it " that shadowed his life, that weighed constantly on his sensitive soul — he hobbled off to the porch where he settled himself in the hammock and began to read. From the living-room within he could hear his mother's voice talking with a caller. He did not listen at first, but just as he was turning the page the caller's words struck his ear.

" Then it's really true? "

" Yes," his mother answered, " it's true, but Mr. Randall does not want anything said about it just yet. We haven't even told the boys."

Eddie strained his ears to find out what it was all about.

" When? " asked the visitor.

" The first of next month."

" So soon? It seems too bad."

" Yes, indeed," sighed Mrs. Randall. " I suppose it is all for the best, but I just hate the thought of it."

The caller departed, and Eddie lay back in the hammock, his book for once forgotten, pondering over the words he had overheard. In the unknown there is always anxiety. He wondered and wondered what they had been discussing. What was it that was going to happen on the first of the month that dad did not wish to talk about? It must be something that did not please his mother. She had said

that she hated the thought of it. Vague fears
began to fill his brain. He wondered if it was
anything that had to do with him. He wondered if they were going to send him away anywhere. He had read only the other day in the
newspaper of a " Home for Incurables." Perhaps they had come to the conclusion that his
leg was never going to be any better and were
going to put him in some such place.

No, he decided, it could not be that. Mother
loved him. She never would let him go to a
home for incurables, even if his leg did not get
well. He racked his brain for other solutions
of the mystery. It was beyond him. He
thought of reporting the conversation to his
brothers to see if they could make anything out
of it, but something inside him warned him
against any such procedure. He felt that it
had not been quite honorable for him to listen
to a conversation not intended for his ears.
He felt sure it would be still less honorable for
him to repeat what he had heard. He decided
it would be best for him to tell mother about it
when she came to kiss him good night. Yet at
bedtime Mrs. Randall seemed to be so absorbed
in her own thoughts that he did not find opportunity.

What was it that was going to happen?
What was the dire thing in prospect on the first
of the month that his mother just hated to
think of. Eddie hardly slept all night long,
it worried him so.

Next morning at breakfast the mystery was
cleared up. Dad sat down to the table looking
entirely free from worry and just like his old
self.

"Boys," he announced cheerily, "I've some
news for you. We're going to move."

They looked at him in blank amazement.
The idea was too novel, too stupendous, for
them to grasp at once. In all their debating
they never had given thought to such a possibility as this.

"What do you mean?" asked Tom at length.
"Going to move into another house?"

People in the town where the Randalls lived
were not in the habit of moving. Once the
Wilsons had built a new house and had moved
into it, leaving their former dwelling to a married son. Another time that Tom recalled a
family had gone out West, and their old home
had remained untenanted. Moving was something wholly new and unfamiliar, and he was
not quite sure he welcomed the idea. This was

home. The three boys had been born in the house and always had lived there.

"No," his father explained, "not just to another house. We're going to move to another town — to the city, in fact."

There was a note of pride in his tone as he spoke. For years he had dreamed of this — of moving to the city, of a larger practice, of more opportunities, of greater advantages, and now it was to come true.

"Oh, great!" cried Richard. The soul of the adventurer was his. His affection for people and places was not so deep-rooted as in the others. He welcomed change of any sort.

Eddie was silent. Into his eyes came great tears. He felt like crying. The prospect of leaving his home, of going off to a strange place, among people he did not know, of leaving forever the house, the barn, the school, did not appeal to him in the least.

"Why can't we stay here?" he stammered. "I don't want to move."

His mother's arm reached out protectingly and encircled his shoulder. "That's just the way I feel about it, too, Eddie, dear," she said. "I wish we didn't have to move."

"But why do we?" the boy persisted.

"It's for father's business," Mrs. Randall hastened to explain. "He has been offered the place as lawyer for a big insurance company, and it means, Eddie, dear, that he is going to make a lot more money, and now we can afford to have a big New York doctor examine your leg and see if he can not do something so that you will not be lame any more. Won't that be nice?"

Eddie gulped down a sob. "Don't move on my account," he said plaintively. "I don't mind being lame — that is I don't mind it very much."

"It's all settled," announced Mr. Randall briskly. "We're going to move on the first of the month. I'll be very busy at the office getting things straightened up, so you boys can stay at home from school for the next few days and help mother and Maggie with the packing."

"That'll be fine," cried Tom.

"Great," echoed Richard.

Eddie alone was silent. He was sure that he abhorred the whole idea. He did not want to move. He did not want to stay home from school. Tom and Richard did not like their lessons, but he did. He had a perfect attendance record of which he was very proud, a record that contained only one blot — the time he had been suspended because he would not tell on some of the other boys. And besides there was "The Prize"! One of the school directors had offered ten dollars in gold for the pupil who passed the best examination in American history. He had said little about it at home, but he had made up his mind to win it. What if he could not run like other boys? What if he was not any good in most of the games they played? There was nothing the matter with his head. He would show everybody that he could win at something. He had set his heart on this prize. And now, if they moved away, he would lose all chance of getting it.

"Do I have to stay home from school?" he asked his mother, after Dad had gone to the office.

"Why no, of course not," his mother answered. "I want Tom and Richard to help me, but you would not be able to help mother very much anyhow, so run along to school if you want to."

Little did busy Mrs. Randall realize that her way of putting it had cut Eddie to the heart.

He knew he was not much use in running errands and beating carpets, but it hurt so to have even his mother speak of it in that way.

Sorrowfully he set out for school, taking little interest in the jubilant and important air with which his brothers prepared to help in packing up. All the week he was as one aloof from the family, returning from school each day to find further evidence of a dismantled home. The carpets and rugs had been taken up, the piano had been crated, and all the contents of the attic sorted out. Tom and Richard were jubilant over the discovery of great heaps of old clothing which their mother announced were not worth taking away with them.

"Can we sell 'em to the ragman?" asked Dick.

"Anything to get rid of them," Mrs. Randall answered.

"And can we keep the money?" asked Tom.

"Yes, if you divide what you get with Eddie," had been her reply.

The sorting out of the attic's treasure-trove had been a source of much pleasure to Tom and Richard and the other boys of their acquaintance.

" Tell you what," said Fatty Bullen, " we'll get a couple of bricks and wrap a lot of old rags about them and put them in the middle of each bag and that'll make them weigh a lot heavier. I did that once and got lots and lots more money."

" Great," said Tom.

" Bully idea," said Dick.

" That would be cheating," objected Eddie.

" No," said Tom, " the ragman 'd cheat us if he could. I've often heard mother say he was an old cheat anyhow."

" Sure," said Dick, " he'd cheat us if he could."

" You bet he would," asserted Fatty. " 'Tain't cheating. All the fellers do it."

Eddie was unconvinced. He would have liked to ask his mother about it, but somehow it seemed almost like tattling. He decided to say nothing.

" Go on and do it if you want to," he announced, " but I say it's cheating. If you do, I'm not going to take any of the money."

" You can do as you please about that," retorted Tom.

" You don't have to take it if you don't want

to," said Dick, already beginning to figure how much they would have if what the ragman paid them was divided by two instead of three.

Their summary manner of eliminating him only added to Eddie's burden. He had hoped that they would leave out the bricks and insist on his taking his share. Maybe he was wrong about it. Maybe it wasn't cheating. Still he was not going to weaken.

"All right," he announced, "leave me out of it."

Despondently he left the boys and went off to see old Jonas.

"Mr. Jonas," he asked, "did you ever move?"

"No," the old one-legged shopkeeper replied. "I can't rightfully say that I have. That little house over there where I live is the house where I was born. Of course, when I was away soldiering, I did a lot of moving, living sometimes in barracks and sometimes in tents, but you'd hardly call that moving."

"Our folks are going to move," announced Eddie gloomily.

"You don't say. Where they going to move to — to another part of town?"

"No, they're going to move to the city."

" Well, now," said Jonas, " that's kind of nice, isn't it ? "

Like all persons who have spent their lives in smaller places, the city to him had a fascination. Handicapped as he was with his wooden leg, with all his seventy years save the few he had served as a soldier spent in the same little town, seeing the same people every day, doing the same things every week, he often had meditated on life in larger places and had felt that he would like to participate in it.

" I don't think it's a bit nice. I was away for a whole week once at Aunt Carrie's, and it isn't a bit comfortable being anywhere else than home. Everything's different when you're away. And I won't be able to come and see you any more, either."

" I'll miss you a lot," the old man answered, his eyes dimming a little at the thought. The boy's friendship was one of the few bright spots in his lonely life. He looked forward each day to the little fellow's visit. " But I don't see how it can be helped. If your folks have made up their mind to go, that's all there is to it."

" But they never asked me whether I wanted to or not," cried Eddie. " Nobody cares any-

For once old Jonas was at a loss to know how to comfort him.
Page 275.

thing about what I like. I'm working for the history prize in school and I'll lose that and everything."

For once old Jonas was at a loss to know how to comfort him.

"There, there, Eddie," he said consolingly, "maybe you'll like the new place better'n you do this."

"I won't! I know I won't! I couldn't like it. It won't be home."

"I don't see what can be done about it."

"Well," said Eddie desperately, "I'm just not going to do it, that's all. The rest of them can move if they want to. I'm not going to move; I'm going to stay right here at home."

A sudden solution of his new problem had come to him. So occupied was he with his idea that something of the morbidness with which he had looked on the preparations for moving left him. When the next afternoon mother informed him that it was time for him to pack up the things in his room, he set about the task cheerfully, and when he had gone upstairs, Mrs. Randall paused in her work to remark to Maggie: "Eddie is getting used to the idea of moving, I guess. He seemed heart-broken at first."

" Yes'm," said Maggie, " it don't take boys long to get used to anything. It's different with us folks."

If they could have read the thoughts of the morbid youngster on the floor above, they might not have been so confident about his change of mind. " They none of them care about me," Eddie was saying to himself. " They never asked me whether I wanted to move or not. They none of them care whether I win the prize."

The more he sympathized with himself the more bitter he became. His packing did not take long and he wandered idly about the dismantled house, every one else too busy with final preparations to pay any attention to him. He passed from room to room, viewing the bareness of each with a sinking heart, and after several surreptitious visits to the kitchen was mysteriously missing for nearly half an hour.

Shortly before noon mother called him upstairs and bade him don his best suit, hardly waiting until he had put off his every-day clothes before she jammed them into a trunk.

They had lunch standing up around a great dry-goods box, eating cold meat off wooden platters with their fingers, for all the dishes and knives and forks had been packed. Even while they were eating the men with the express-wagon came to take the box and the trunks away. Most of the furniture had gone the day before.

"Our train goes at two-thirty," Mrs. Randall reminded the boys, "so if you want to go to say good-by to any of your friends, you may do so, but be sure to be back here by a quarter of two."

Quickly Tom and Richard dashed off together as usual, leaving Eddie behind them. He hobbled out of the house toward the barn, and then with a furtive glance to see that no one was observing him he passed around the back of the building. A quarter of two came. Tom and Richard dashed up the street, arriving just a minute before their father, who had made a last visit to his office. The bags and bundles had all been assembled on the porch. Mrs. Randall came out of the house with her hat and coat on.

"Where's Eddie?" she asked.

No one could recall having seen him for fully an hour.

"Run out to the barn and see if he is there," Mr. Randall suggested to Richard.

Mrs. Randall reopened the door of the deserted house and called his name aloud. There was no response. Dick came back and reported that there was no sign of him in the barn.

"Oh, dear," exclaimed Mrs. Randall, "the carriage will be here any minute to take us to the station. I wonder where he can be."

"I expect he's off saying good-by to that old Jonas he's so fond of," said Mr. Randall. "Tom, you run down and see if he is there."

Meanwhile they waited and waited. The carriage came. Mr. Randall began looking at his watch. Mrs. Randall and Maggie rushed about the place, frantically calling Eddie's name, running out every few minutes to see if Tom was coming up the street.

"We'll have to start in three minutes if we're going to make that train," Mr. Randall announced just as Tom returned breathless.

"Old Jonas says he hasn't seen him since yesterday," he reported.

Mrs. Randall gasped and turned white. "Where can Eddie be? What can have happened to him?" she cried, recalling now for the first time how little attention she had paid to her lame son in the last few days.

"If he doesn't turn up in the next two minutes, we'll go off without him," announced her husband wrathfully. "He knew what time the train went, and there's no excuse for his not being here. Here, boys, you and Maggie get in and take these bags."

"Something's happened to Eddie," asserted his mother in panic. "He's always on time."

"Come, get in," said Mr. Randall, looking at his watch for the twentieth time, "we've got to start."

"William Randall," exclaimed his wife, "if you think I'm going one step without Eddie, you're much mistaken. I'm going to wait right here till I find out what's happened to him."

"We'll all miss the train," stormed Mr. Randall.

"The rest of you go on," said his wife. "Give me two of the tickets, and I'll come when I find Eddie."

So that was the way they settled it. There was hardly time for good-by kisses for the other two boys. Off the carriage started.

"When you find him," Mr. Randall called out, "telegraph what train you are coming on, and I'll meet you."

Left to herself on the porch of the empty house, Mrs. Randall debated what she should do first. She tried to make herself believe that Eddie had lingered somewhere in the neighborhood and hesitated about leaving the house lest he should return and find every one gone. Fortunately, in the hurry of departure the keys had been left with her. She unlocked the front door, and leaving it open went from room to room, peering into every corner and calling Eddie's name. At last, satisfied that he could be nowhere in the house, she locked the door again. She made a hasty inspection of the yard, the barn, the porches. Nowhere was there a sign of Eddie.

Her fears now began to be more acute. She ran to the next-door neighbor's and called for help, excitedly telling of Eddie's mysterious disappearance. Soon almost every one in the town knew that Eddie Randall was missing and was helping in the search. Even the constable was notified and put up a notice in the post-office. Not until darkness fell could Mrs. Randall be persuaded to give up her frantic search and go to a neighbor's house for rest and refreshment, even then the only argument that had prevailed with her having been the advice that she must keep up her strength to aid in the search. Nor would she consent to leave the house until she had been promised that some one would stay on watch on the porch in case Eddie should come home.

Meanwhile, where was Eddie?

When he left the house at noon that day, he had a well-formulated plan in his mind. Growing more and more grieved and morbid at the idea of leaving home, of giving up all chance of winning the history prize, he had deliberately decided to remain behind. Two days before, he had selected a hiding-place, the old dry-goods box at the end of the garden which had once been the home of the rabbits. He was going to stay there in hiding until after the family had gone, and then he would go and live with old Jonas. He had said nothing to Jonas about it, but he was sure the old man would take him in, and then he would keep on going to school and would get the prize — it would be awarded next week — and then — well, then, while he had not looked that far ahead, he was sort of picturing a triumphal return to the bosom of the family that had neglected to consult his wishes about moving. He just could see himself displaying that ten-

dollar gold-piece, and ouldn't Tom and Richard be jealous of him   Let them move if they
wanted to.

As a precaution against hunger and thirst he
had smuggled out of the kitchen a bottle of
milk, a loaf of bread, some butter, an old
kitchen-knife, and some ginger cookies.   These
he had hidden safely under a pile of dried grass
in the rabbit-pen.

Dressed in his best, he had slipped away from
the house and crawled into the pen, carefully
covering himself with the heap of grass.

How long he had been hiding he had no idea.
From time to time he heard voices calling him.
He listened with amusement when he heard
Tom and Richard, but by and by at the sound
of his mother's voice, a sense of desolation and
loneliness came over him.   It was all he could
do to refrain from answering her.   Still, if he
did, he would have to move away and would
forever lose the prize.   He snuggled still farther into the dried grass and kept still.   By
and by, when all was quiet, he ventured to eat
some of the cookies.   He tried to drink the
milk, but it had soured.   He became thirstier
and thirstier.   The bits of grass tickled him.
His feet went to sleep.   He grew more and

more uncomfortable. He began to doubt the wisdom of his course. He wanted his mother. He began to cry softly, and then he fell asleep.

It was hours afterward when he awoke with a start. It was pitch dark, and at first he could not think where he was or what had happened. Then he remembered. He scrambled hastily out of his hiding place and emerged from the rabbit-pen. Trembling with fear in the darkness, his first thought had been to run to the house, but as he looked toward it and saw it looming up, a dark unfamiliar shape, he remembered that there was nobody there, that they had moved away, all of them — all but him.

In the sense of utter desolation that came over him he wanted to shriek aloud, but he did not dare. Where was he to go? What could he do? Like a ray of light in the darkness came the thought of old Jonas. At least he hadn't moved away. With fearful feet he stumbled through the deserted garden and out to the sidewalk and hobbled as fast as he could down toward the tracks where the tobacco-shop was. The streets were deserted, most of the searchers having gone home for supper. There were lights still in some of the windows, but to the terrified youngster it seemed as if it must be late, very late, maybe midnight. As he hobbled along the street, a new panic seized him. What if Jonas wasn't at his shop? What if he had gone home to bed? He was not sure he could find the house in the dark. And maybe, too, he would not be able to arouse Jonas.

"If mother was only here!" he kept saying over and over again to himself.

As he approached the tobacco-shop, he saw with delight that the door stood open and a light shone forth. He tried to run, but stumbled and fell. By the time he got to his feet the light had gone out and he could just see dimly the form of old Jonas locking up his shop for the night.

"Oh, Mr. Jonas!" he managed to shriek and then toppled over again as he tried once more to run.

Fortunately his friend had heard him and came hobbling toward him as fast as his wooden leg would let him.

"Why, Eddie," he exclaimed, "where have you been? The whole town has been hunting you."

"I didn't want to move," sobbed Eddie,

clutching Jonas' hand with a sigh of relief, "and I went and hid in the rabbit-pen and I fell asleep and when I woke up all my folks were gone away."

"No, your mother wouldn't go without you. She's still here," announced Jonas.

"Where is she?"

"You come right here in the shop and lie down," said old Jonas, "and I'll get her here pretty quick."

Unlocking the shop-door and lighting up, he made Eddie lie down on a bench there and despatched a passing boy for Mrs. Randall. While they awaited her arrival, Eddie told the whole story, how he did not want to move, and how his heart was set on winning the history prize.

"And did you tell your mother about the prize?" asked Jonas.

"No-o, not exactly," said Eddie, "I wanted to surprise her."

"Well, then, you see," explained Jonas, "it was all your own fault. Even mothers can't always read what's going on in a boy's mind. If your mother'd known about that prize, I'll bet she'd have found a way. Mothers generally do."

" Yes," admitted Eddie, " they do."

" And I guess you've learned by now," admonished old Jonas, " since you've looked at that empty dark building where you used to live that a boy's home is something more than just a house."

" You bet," said Eddie, as he turned to greet his mother, " home's where mother is."

It was late the next afternoon when Mr. Randall met his wife at the train.

" Where's Eddie? " he asked in amazement.

" I left him behind with old Jonas," she answered smilingly. " He's going to school a week longer to win the history prize."

" Didn't he want to come home with you? " asked Mr. Randall incredulously.

" Yes and no," said Mrs. Randall, borrowing one of Jonas' pet phrases and smiling happily to herself at the thought that at any rate she and Eddie understood.

CHAPTER THIRTEEN

IN A STRANGE LAND

THE brakeman thrust his head in the door and bawled something utterly unintelligible. A small lame boy, all alone in a car seat, once more consulted a crumpled schedule and strained his eyes trying to ascertain the name printed on the station at which the train had stopped.

Edward Haverford Randall was making his first train journey and making it all alone. The boy was tired, for he had been up since five o'clock in the morning and it had been an eventful day. After a hasty breakfast in the cottage old Jonas had insisted on accompanying him to the station to see him safely on the train.

"Mr. Jonas," Eddie had asked as they approached the station, "do you suppose the boys in the city'll call me 'Limpy' as they do here?"

"They're apt to do just that," the old man

replied, shaking his head sadly. "Boys is boys everywhere, not given to caring much about hurting people's feelings."

"Well, I don't mind — much," answered Eddie bravely.

"That's the way to take it," said his friend approvingly. "Let them call you anything they've a mind to. You just up and show them you're not lame in the head, even if you've only a leg and a half."

"That's just what I'm going to do," announced Eddie with a brave air of determination.

So all the way on the long train trip, as he looked out of the window, as he watched the other passengers, as he listened to the brakeman calling the stations, as he ate the luncheon old Jonas had provided, all the time he kept trying to think of ways and means of demonstrating to the new boys he was soon to meet that he wasn't lame in the head. It was not that Eddie had any unreasonable desire to show off. It is as much a part of boy nature as it is of manhood ambition, to wish to excel. Every boy likes to be best at something. On Eddie's limited horizon there seemed to be so little in which there was any likelihood of his excelling. To be sure he was better at his studies than either of his older brothers, Tom and Richard. He could beat both of them — and even Dad, sometimes — at checkers. Yet somehow these were not the sort of things that boys appreciated, though it was here that Eddie's accomplishments ended. He could not run nor jump nor swim nor climb, nor do any of the things that boys cared most about.

What was there for him to do in order to show these new boys? It seemed almost a hopeless task. He felt himself becoming more and more discouraged at the prospect. He resolutely set his jaw. He must not give up. He must find some way. He must do something. What should it be?

Once more the train stopped. The afternoon was waning. He evidently was approaching his destination. Anxiously he studied the schedule, reading for the fiftieth time the list of stations to make sure that he knew where the train had stopped. The next station must be where he got off. A sudden feeling of fear smote him. What if there should be no one there to meet him? He would not know where to go. With a queer sinking of the heart he realized that he did not know

where his home was now.   Old Jonas had said
that he would send a telegram after the train
started, but suppose something had happened!
Suppose old Jonas forgot, or the telegram had
not been delivered! They would not even
know he was coming.

As the train stopped in the terminal station
he clambered down the steps, looking anxiously
about, utterly bewildered by the noise and confusion, and feeling very much alone.   It was
his mother who spied him first and as he heard
her joyous cry of greeting he saw with glad
eyes the little group gathered to welcome him
— Mother and Dad, his two brothers, and even
Maggie.   A moment later he was clasped in
his mother's arms and was the target for a
volley of questions:

" How's Mother's precious? "

" Well, young man, how did you stand the
trip? "

" Weren't you afraid, coming all by yourself? "

" Bless the boy, did he have something to
eat? "— this from Maggie, ever mindful of his
physical welfare.

" Say, Eddie, did you win that ten dollars? "

It was his brother Richard of course who

asked the latter question.   Already he was devising plans for helping Eddie spend the
money.

From his arrival, until he went to bed at
nine, life was a wonderful round of excitement.   It was not a carriage that they entered
outside the station but a taxicab, with a register
that kept clicking off dimes every few blocks.
The house at which it finally stopped — Eddie's new home,— looked very odd to him.   It
had no yard about it at all.   It was
one of a row of neat brick houses that to
Eddie's small-town eye looked exactly alike.
Within the house, too, there were many fea-
tures novel to him to be explored and in the
rear there was a yard, a tiny bit of a yard, surrounded by a high board fence, and a clothes
horse with arms that folded up.   In the bath-
room there was a shower bath which Tom and
Richard hastened to demonstrate to Eddie's
wondering eye, and in the dining-room and the
living-room were all sorts of interesting but-
tons, by which you could turn the electric lights
on in sections.

Of course, too, he had to inspect the room he
was to occupy,— *his* room.   His first sensation was one of disappointment.   It was not

nearly as large as the one he formerly occupied, and it was up on the third floor, away from Mother's room. Tom and Richard, to be sure, were located across the hall, just as formerly, but Eddie as he looked doubtfully about him was not quite sure that he could ever feel at home in the place. Even the sight of his chest with all his treasures waiting for him to unpack them did not wholly alleviate the feeling of abhorrence for his new quarters that he felt creeping over him.

" Do you like your new room, Eddie dear? " asked his mother anxiously.

" Yes, mother," he answered without enthusiasm, and Mrs. Randall turned away satisfied, never dreaming of the wave of mental revolt against his new surroundings that was engulfing her son. It is boy habit, even in cases where there is as strong a bond as that which existed between Eddie and his mother, for a boy to keep to himself his innermost feelings. " Yes," from a youngster means little. It is the easiest answer to make. Experience has taught him that it is the least bothersome way to avoid further questions. He says " Yes " and goes on thinking his own thoughts, fearful of revealing them lest he be laughed at.

Thus it happened that it was not until he went to bed that night that he and mother really had a confidential chat. As she massaged his aching leg he told her all about his week with old Jonas, of how he had won the history prize and what the teacher had said. This time when she asked him: "Are you sure you like your new room?" he told her the truth about it. He confessed to her that he did not like being so far away from her, and that it was too small, and that there was nothing to see from the window but houses, and that he didn't think he ever would be able to get used to it or to get to sleep in it.

"That's just the way I felt about it at first, Eddie," his mother said consolingly. "It did not seem a bit like our dear old home and I felt I never could get accustomed to these tiny rooms."

"I wish we could all move home again," said her son plaintively. "Can't we?"

"Wait a week," said Mrs. Randall cheerily, "and you'll be surprised how quickly you become accustomed to it. Besides as soon as you start to school you'll be too busy to bother."

"How soon do I have to start to school?"

" Next Monday, of course. Don't you want to go? " asked Mrs. Randall in amazement. Eddie had always been the one of her three boys who liked school.

" I don't know."

Mrs. Randall was much puzzled by his manner. She felt that there was something bothering him, yet she was too wise a mother to ask the question direct. After they had talked for five minutes more the trouble was revealed.

" Mother," asked Eddie anxiously," do you s'pose the boys here will call me ' Limpy '? "

" Why, no, of course they won't," she said without hesitation, speaking against probability as her mother heart suddenly comprehended the dread with which her little boy was looking forward to the ordeal of meeting and making the acquaintance with a horde of new boys, unthinking youngsters who would sear his sensitive soul by talking to him about his deformity.

" Don't worry about it at all," she comforted him. " Mother knows it will be all right."

Thus reassured, Eddie kissed her goodnight and almost before she was out of the room was sound asleep.

Mrs. Randall hastened down-stairs to her husband.

"Do you know what has been bothering that poor little chap all evening?" she exclaimed. "He has been worrying his heart out for fear the boys here will call him 'Limpy.'"

"Very likely they will," said Mr. Randall.

"Well, I'm just not going to have it, that's all," she announced wrathfully. "I'm going to write a letter to the principal this very night telling him he must forbid the boys calling my Eddie names."

"Don't do anything foolish," cautioned her husband. "That would only make matters worse. It would put the notion in the heads of a lot of boys who never had thought of it before."

"But I must do something."

"What can you do? Better let a boy fight his own battles."

"You don't want your son called 'Limpy' and eating his heart out in grief because of it, do you?"

"Oh, pooh," said Mr. Randall, turning again to his evening paper, "nicknames don't harm a boy. Mixing with other boys is the best education a youngster can have. It fits him for the knocks he gets in after-life. You make too much of a mama's boy out of Eddie as it is."

"William Randall," exclaimed his wife indignantly, "I don't think you know a thing about boys, even if you were one yourself."

Mr. Randall laughed.

"Go ahead and write your letter. If you do the other boys may not call him 'Limpy,' but it will be 'Mama's pet' or something worse, you'll find. I know boys."

Even though she could not quite agree with her husband's view, Mrs. Randall did not write the note, but when Monday morning came she made ready to accompany Eddie to school, with the full intention of explaining to the principal in person how sensitive her son was about his lameness. To her amazement Eddie himself firmly vetoed her going with him.

"There's no need for your going," he announced. "Tom and Richard'll show me where the principal's room is."

"But — but — I want to tell him about your studies."

"I've got all my last term's report cards," announced Eddie calmly, "and besides the

boys would guy a big fellow like me if he came
to school with his mother."

That settled it. Eddie went off with his
brothers and his mother had a little weeping
spell. Nor were her tears all for Eddie. She
was weeping mostly for herself, from the loneliness of the mother suddenly brought to the
realization that her baby is no longer hers, that
he, without her knowing it, has become a " big
fellow," not nearly so dependent on her as she
had thought him. Eddie — her youngest —
her baby — a big fellow — she could not realize it, and yet as she swallowed back the tears
she felt that henceforth she must.

Brave as was the front Eddie kept up before his mother as he hobbled off with Tom and
Richard, it was with a sinking heart that he
approached the school building. The struc-
ture was much larger than the school in his
home town and he was certain he never would
be able to find his way around in it. Everything looked so different and strange. Perhaps they would put him in a room away up on
the third floor where he would have two flights
of stairs to climb, and that was hard work for
him. Maybe, too, they would insist on his
taking " physical exercise," from which he

hitherto had always been excused on account
of his lameness. He began to wish Mother
was along to explain all these things for him.

As they entered the school gate his brothers
deserted him.

" That's Professor Hilder's room there, the
first one on the left," explained Tom.

" Old Hilder's getting bald and wears
specs," added Richard.

Bewildered at being left alone, for he had
expected that his brothers at least would introduce him to the principal, Eddie timidly
entered the building, striving to hide his limp
as he went up the steps. At the main door he
paused and peered timidly within. Perhaps
he might be able to find the place. There
right in front of him stood a door invitingly
open on which was " Office of the Principal."
Still he stood hesitating. He dreaded to go
in alone. He hoped that some one would
come along and go into the room and then he
could follow them. No one came by. He
heard the five-minute bell ring and mustered
up his courage and entered. A pleasant-
faced man with spectacles was sitting at a desk
examining some papers. He did not look up
at first and Eddie stood silently in front of

his desk not knowing just what to do and getting all trembly as he waited.

" Well, my boy," said the principal at length, " what is it? "

Eddie tried to speak. His mouth seemed suddenly to dry up. The words he tried to say sank away back in his throat and choked him. He began to tremble more violently and the terrible fear came over him that he was going to disgrace himself by crying, though what he would be crying for he could not tell.

" What is your name? " asked Professor Hilder.

" Ed — Ed — Eddie Randall," he managed to say. He had pictured himself as announcing his full name but somehow he could not enunciate it.

" Oh," said the principal, " you're a new pupil, a brother of those boys who entered last week, are you? "

Eddie nodded mutely and extended his report cards, managing to gain a little better control of himself as the principal examined the documents.

" H-m, h-m," said Professor Hilder, " good, very good. Let me see, I think we will start you in 5A."

A wave of joy swept over the youngster at the announcement, obliterating all other emotions for the moment. Even in his confusion he realized he was receiving promotion far beyond his dreams. He was skipping two whole grades. At home he had been in 4B.

" That'll be fine," he said with enthusiasm, speaking for the first time in his natural tones.

A minute later he found himself in one of the rooms on the main floor, being introduced to his new teacher.

" Miss Armstrong," said Professor Hilder, " I have brought you a new pupil, Edward Randall, who comes to us with very good reports. He is to be excused from physical exercise."

Miss Armstrong, a plump young woman with a pleasant smile, greeted Eddie cordially, showed him a hook where he was to keep his cap, and guided him to his seat.

" I will not ask you to join any of the classes to-day," she said. " I think you will like it better if you just sit here and watch how we do things and get acquainted."

" That'll be fine," said Eddie. Already he was beginning to be sure that he was going to like both principal and teacher. Professor Hilder had promoted him and had excused him from physical exercise without being asked and Miss Armstrong seemed to have read his thoughts in not calling on him to join his classes just yet.

With attentive eyes and ears he listened to all that went on and studied the difference in methods and observed his classmates. He soon decided that he would have no difficulty in keeping up with the others and turned his attention to studying the other boys who were also studying him. He felt glad that he was sitting down so that they would not notice his lameness. As he became accustomed to his surroundings his self-possession returned. He decided he was going to like his new school as much as he had the other one.

Almost before he realized it the session was over and he had taken his place in line to march out of the room.

"How'd you hurt your leg?" whispered the boy with whom he was mated.

"I didn't," answered Eddie calmly, "it grew that way."

Eddie himself could not understand it. The reference to his lameness, about which he ordinarily had been so sensitive, this time had not embarrassed him in the least.

"Gee, that's tough," said the other boy sympathetically.

"Aw, I don't mind it," replied Eddie. "The other kids call me 'Limpy' but I don't care."

"They call me 'Four-eyed,'" announced the other, who wore glasses.

"Why," exclaimed Eddie delightedly, "I know a kid at home we called the same name — Four-eyed Smith."

"My name's McCollough — they call me Four-eyed Mac," said his new acquaintance.

"And I'm Limpy Randall — my real name's Eddie — Edward Haverford Randall."

Outside the building their ways separated.

"So long, Limpy, see you 's afternoon," called out the McCollough boy.

"So long, Four-eyed," cried Eddie as he hastened home to relate to his anxious mother the events of the morning while he ate his luncheon.

"And did any of the boys call you 'Limpy'?" she inquired anxiously after Tom and Richard had left the table.

" Sure," said Eddie, carelessly, to her great bewilderment, " I told them to call me that. All the fellows have nicknames."

Puzzled beyond words by this new attitude of her youngest toward his infirmity, Mrs. Randall continued her questions. She wanted to know if he had had any difficulty in getting excused from physical exercise.

" No," said Eddie, offering no details, " I fixed that all right," going on to tell how he had skipped two whole grades, and hurrying away to school again before half his mother's questions had been answered.

" I guess William is right," she said to herself thoughtfully, as she watched Eddie until he was out of sight. " I don't believe I do understand boys. Here I was all worked up for fear the other boys would call him ' Limpy ' and he comes home and calmly tells me that he has told them to call him that. It beats me."

Meanwhile Eddie at school was having new and interesting experiences. At the afternoon session he took part in all the classes, acquitting himself creditably in spite of the fact that he had not studied a single one of the lessons. An hour before the session ended

Miss Armstrong made a novel announcement.

" Boys," she said, " the girls in Miss Rider's room — 5A — think they are better spellers than you are. They have challenged you to a spelling match. It is to take place in the Assembly Room. You will march in there quietly and take your places along the west wall. Whenever one of you misses a word he will have to sit down. When one of the girls misses she will sit down. The room that has the most still in line at four o'clock will be the winner."

A spelling match was a novelty to Eddie. They did not have them in the school he formerly had attended. As the other pupils took their places in line to march into the Assembly Room he still sat in his place wondering whether or not he was expected to take part in it. Miss Armstrong noticed his hesitation.

" Randall," she said, " as this is your first day here you may be excused —" then observing the look of disappointment that flashed across his face she added quickly, " that is, unless you want to take part. I see you have very good reports in spelling."

" I think I'd like it very much," said Eddie getting up quickly to march in with the others.

In the Assembly Room he found that as became a new arrival he had a place down near the end of the line. He was glad of that. It would give him time to collect his thoughts and to observe what the others did before he was called upon to spell any words. After they had all taken their places, the girls from Miss Rider's room in one aisle and the boys from Miss Armstrong's classes in the aisle opposite, facing them, Professor Hilder came in and began giving out words, first to a boy and then to a girl and so on down the line. If a boy missed a word the next boy in the line had a chance to spell it. If he failed, the word was put to the girls' line.

Eddie found it exceedingly interesting and exciting. The words thus far given out had a familiar sound and he was certain they were from the same spelling book they had used in his old school. This gave him no small feeling of satisfaction, for he was certain that he could spell correctly every word it contained.

At first there were very few misses. Professor Hilder seemed to be selecting the words from the front part of the book where all the pupils were on familiar territory. With his face flushed from the excitement Eddie

eagerly awaited his turn. The boy next to
him went down on " cemetery," putting in two
" m's." Eddie spelled it correctly and soon
the head of the line was reached again. The
principal now turned to the back of the book
and began skipping around and the list of
casualties rapidly increased. Two girls and
two boys got flustered over " gerrymander."
They tried to spell it with a " j," with one
" r," with an " i " instead of a " y," with two
" m's "— every way but the right way, until
at last Eddie's new friend, " Four-eyed Mac "
saved the day for the boys by getting it cor-
rect.

One by one they were falling out now on
both sides. Eleven words had come to Eddie
and each of them he had spelled correctly without any hesitation. The lines were fast growing shorter and Eddie, as his unsuccessful
mates took their seats, found himself moving
step by step up nearer the head. Soon there
were left only four of the girls and three of the
boys. Two of the girls and one of the boys
went down on " renaissance." On the boys'
side there were left now only " Four-eyed
Mac " and Eddie. The girls' side was still
headed by a petite vision in blue with golden

brown curls and brown eyes and pretty red lips — Diana Wallace her name was, Eddie had learned from the whispered conversation about him. Thus far she had spelled every word correctly as had Nellie Curtis, a slender dark elf with snapping black eyes, who stood beside her.

Eddie, looking across the aisle at his opponents, found himself wishing that Diana would win. She was ever and ever so much prettier than the other little girl, he decided, prettier even than little Floribel Finch. As each new word was put to Nellie Curtis he began hoping that she would fail on it so that only Diana would be left. For a long time Nellie seemed invincible but at last his wish came true.

" Rhetorician," enunciated Professor Hilder.

" R-e-t-o-r-i-c-i-a-n " spelled the Curtis girl confidently.

" Wrong," said Professor Hilder, " McCollough — rhetorician."

He was giving out the words turn about, first to a girl and then to a boy, now that there were left only the four of them. Nellie Curtis, striving hard to keep back the tears, reluctantly took her seat and "Four-eyed Mac" with a triumphant glance in her direction essayed the word.

He made the fatal error of trying to give it two " t's " and a second later Eddie and Diana Wallace faced each other, sole surviving champions of their rooms.

A wave of exultation swept over Eddie. He had been hoping vainly for an opportunity to demonstrate to these new boys that he wasn't lame in the head. He had promised old Jonas that he would do it somehow. All unsought his great opportunity had come. Already he had spelled down every boy in the room. It only remained to vanquish the girl opposite. He felt that his victory was assured. As the contest went on he had been gaining in self-assurance. He felt certain that he could outspell any girl that lived. Sooner or later she would trip on some word and then he would be the winner.

He shot a triumphant glance across the aisle at his opponent and had a change of heart. A wavering doubt crept into his mind. Maybe it would be nicer to let her win. Probably she was just as eager as he to be the victor. Perhaps she might cry if she didn't win. He de-

cided that he would not like to make her cry.
Still he wanted so much to win himself. He
just had to show the new boys that he
amounted to something even if he was lame.
He must win! Think how proud Mother
would be of him if he did and what fun it
would be to write to old Jonas and tell him
about it!

Meanwhile, as the conflict raged within him,
he kept mechanically spelling the words Professor Hilder was giving out — ten words,
twenty words, thirty words, and still neither
of them had missed. The principal paused
and looked at his watch.

"It is nearly four o'clock," he said, "perhaps we had better call it a draw."

"Please go on," called out one of the girls.

"Yes, yes, go on," cried all the pupils.

Both sides of the room were tense with excitement as boys and girls, aroused by the
spirit of contest, eagerly awaited the outcome.
Once more he began giving out words. Eddie
was getting tired standing. His lame leg was
aching but he hardly minded it at all so eager
was his interest and so confident was he of his
ability to win.

And yet — did he want to? He stole another look at Diana Wallace's eager, sparkling eyes, at her red cheeks, at her pretty curls —

"Randall," said Professor Hilder, "side-real."

Eddie hesitated. He looked across the aisle again at Diana's flushed eager face. A sudden resolution seized him.

"S-i-d-i-r-e-a-l," he spelled almost defiantly.

Professor Hilder paused as if tempted to give him another trial. Miss Armstrong gave a little gasp of disappointment.

"Wrong," said the principal, "Diana, can you spell it?"

"S-i-d-e-r-e-a-l," spelled Diana, bubbling over with happiness as she realized that victory was hers.

A moment later they were both surrounded by their mates, congratulating them on their achievement. With mingled feelings of regret and complacency Eddie listened to the plaudits of his teacher and the boys, even though it was evident that there was a shade of disappointment in their congratulations, that they felt he had betrayed them in the last ditch after so nearly carrying their flag to victory. Yet in the midst of it all he found sweet satisfaction in the knowledge that it was

Diana Wallace who had defeated him. He joyed in his secret that he could have won if he had wished to, and most of all was the sweetly consoling glance Diana gave him as she passed him on the way to her room.

And Eddie's father, happening a few minutes later to pass the school building, stood stock still in astonishment, as a mob of small boys poured forth, headed by a spectacled youngster, and all shouting at the top of their voices as they reached the school yard:

"Hurrah for Limpy Randall."

From the cheering throng as he watched, his youngest son emerged with face flushed and hair tousled, and spying his father, hobbled over to join him and walk home with him.

"Oh, Dad," he cried out joyfully," we had a spelling match, our room and Miss Rider's, the boys against the girls, and I won almost. Four-eyed Mac and I — we spelled all the other fellows down and then there was only me left and a girl on the other side and she won."

"Bully for you," said Mr. Randall enthusiastically, "but don't you mind these new boys calling you Limpy?"

"Pooh," said Eddie, "what do I care for

that? All the fellows in our bunch have nick-names."

And Mr. Randall smiled understandingly, realizing that as Eddie grew older it was beginning to dawn on him that a boy with a lame leg isn't so much different from other boys after all.

CHAPTER FOURTEEN

FOR VALUE RECEIVED

THE three Randall boys had gone to bed. Their parents were seated in the living-room with the windows all wide open, for it was one of those warm autumn evenings when summer's heat seems to be making one last desperate struggle to survive. All up and down the street outside their neighbors, in shirt-waists and shirt-sleeves, were trying to keep cool out on the stoops of the houses, a city habit the Randalls had not yet acquired.

All of them still missed the big wide porch of their village home that had been their favorite idling place. Sitting out on the stoop where all the neighbors could overhear what you were talking about unless you were careful to lower your voice seemed to them too shamelessly public and the evening, after the boys had gone to bed, was really the only time that Mr. and Mrs. Randall ever had for confidential talks.

" There's something I've been wanting to ask you," began Mrs. Randall.

Her husband caught the worried note in her tone and looked up at her perplexedly. He knew that she still pined for the associations and friends of their former home and wondered if it could be that she was dissatisfied. More than likely though, he decided, she had discovered some new mischief on the part of the boys.

" What is it? " he asked.

" It's about Eddie," said his wife hesitatingly.

" Oh, is that all? " he answered with a feeling of relief. " What about him? "

" About his lameness."

" Well," said Mr. Randall, " what about it? It's not getting any worse. He's getting along splendidly now since he has discovered that it does not pay him to mope about it. He doesn't mind now even when the boys call him ' Limpy.' "

" He doesn't seem to care," protested the boy's mother, " but I know he feels just as badly about it as ever, but I was not thinking about that. I was thinking about our promise."

"Our promise!" exclaimed Mr. Randall in surprise. "I do not recall making any promise."

"Don't you remember we told him— when he did not want to move to the city — at least I told him, that the reason we were coming here was so that you could earn money enough that we could afford to have a surgeon operate on his leg."

"Oh, he's forgotten all about that by now. He hasn't said anything about it, has he?"

"No," admitted Mrs. Randall, "he hasn't. But I know he hasn't forgotten."

"Well then, what of it?"

"How soon do you think we can afford it?"

"Not for a long time yet. Moving here cost us quite a lot and I had my new office to furnish up. We had to get a lot of things for the house, too. Living here costs us more than it did formerly, and besides you'll have to get yourself a lot of new duds this fall."

"I don't want any new gowns," said Mrs. Randall almost fiercely, "I'd far rather have Eddie cured than anything else in the world."

"There, there," said her husband soothingly,

" we'll get around to it sooner or later. Just
be patient."

"It's hard to be patient," sighed Mrs. Randall. " I know Eddie far better than you do.
I know how sensitive he is. While he does not
say much even to me I know how much he
suffers from his lameness and how he misses
not being able to do things other boys do and
how he hates to have people talk about his
limping."

"Well," said her husband, firmly, "I
haven't the money now and I will not be able
to spare it this fall and that is all there is to
it."

When he spoke in that tone his wife had
learned from experience that there was little
use in talking further with him. If she attempted to argue with him he would only become more stubborn. She tried to solace herself with the hope that Eddie had forgotten
about her promise. She dreaded his asking
her about it and wondered how best she could
explain to him. From her other sons she
learned that all the boys at school called their
brother " Limpy " most of the time.

"He don't seem to mind it as much as he
used to, though," said Tom.

"I should say not," added Richard, "but he ought to be good and used to it by now. He's always been called that."

She would have liked to question Eddie himself but somehow he seemed to be growing away from her. His bed-time confidences now were by no means as detailed as they formerly had been.

"If we don't do something pretty soon," she said to herself in desperation, "Eddie will be too old. His bones will be getting hardened up and it will be too late for any operation to be successful."

Each day she tried to muster up courage to broach the subject to her husband, yet day by day went by without her having done so. Then one evening her husband came home with a sparkle in his eye and told her he had good news of some sort to impart. She forbore to ask him what it was until after the boys had gone to bed. After she came downstairs after kissing them good-night, Mr. Randall opened up the conversation.

"Whom do you think came to my office to-day to see me?" he asked.

"I have no idea.   Who was it?"

"Mr. Henry Wallace."

"I do not think I ever heard you mention him. Who is he?"

"He's the father of that little girl that was in the spelling match with Eddie, the one whom he nearly spelled down."

"Is that so? What did he want?" asked Mrs. Randall, now vastly more interested as she found that her husband's story apparently involved one of her boys rather than business.

"It's a funny story," Mr. Randall went on. "You see on that day Diana Wallace went home and told how she had won the spelling match from a new boy at school, a little lame boy named Randall. The curious part of it was she insisted to her parents that he had let her win on purpose. She said she just knew our Eddie could have spelled the word he went down on and that she could tell from the way he looked that he did it on purpose."

"The darling!" cried Mrs. Randall enthusiastically. "Isn't that just like him? What a gallant little gentleman he is, and he never said a word to me about it."

"That's not all. Diana's uncle happened to be visiting at their house. He's Dr. Ralston Wallace, the great New York surgeon,

—the man who has done such wonderful things for crippled youngsters. When Diana said the boy was lame he got interested at once. He said to his brother, ' A boy that shows such a fine spirit as that ought not to have to go through life lame. When I get back to New York in about ten days you tell that boy's people to send him on to my new hospital and it won't cost them a cent."

" Oh, isn't that wonderful, simply wonderful! " cried Mrs. Randall, the tears of joy welling up in her eyes.

" It was nice of him," said Mr. Randall. " I thanked him but of course I told him we could not think of accepting the offer. We're not charity patients yet."

" William Randall, you don't mean to tell me you let your foolish pride stand in the way of your little son's being cured. Oh, William, how could you? You *didn't* refuse Mr. Wallace's offer? "

" I did," he admitted rather shamefacedly, " but he wouldn't take no for an answer. He said he was coming in again to see me about it tomorrow."

" You mustn't refuse. You can't," cried his wife. " Don't you see it isn't charity?

It's for value received. Eddie earned it himself by being so kind and chivalrous to that little girl. Don't you see that he did? Eddie's earned it. He must have his chance to be cured. He must. He *must!*"

" I hadn't thought of looking at it that way," said Mr. Randall, as eager as she for his little son's cure despite his masculine way of concealing his real feelings, and welcoming any excuse that would enable him to accept the generous offer without appearing to be a recipient of charity. " I'll see Mr. Wallace again to-morrow."

" And you will let Eddie go to New York, to the hospital?"

" I suppose I must, if that is the way you feel about it."

" Oh, I'm so glad, so very glad."

" But," protested Mr. Randall, " if we do accept you must not let the boys know anything about the arrangement."

Mrs. Randall's face showed her disappointment.

" Can't I even tell Eddie? He won't tell, and I'd like him to know what a wonderful reward his kind action brought to him."

" Not even Eddie," insisted Mr. Randall,

" I don't want the boys to realize yet that their father is a failure."

" Oh, William," cried his wife, " you mustn't feel that way about it. You're just the best husband and the best father that ever lived. And I won't tell a soul. So long as Eddie gets cured, that's all that I care."

As a matter of fact Mr. Randall felt just as badly as she did about Eddie's lameness. It was only that men have a different way from women of showing it when they feel sympathy for any one.   Any kindness toward others — even a kindly thought — a man generally seeks to hide under a gruff manner.   Time and time again Mr. Randall in the privacy of his office had counted up his resources, trying to figure how to stretch his income to make it cover the expense of a specialist's treatment for Eddie. Sometimes he had even contemplated borrowing the amount he would need on his life insurance. The thought that had always deterred him was that after all Eddie was only one of three. He had a duty to the others and to their mother. If anything should happen to him, if he should become ill or disabled, or should die, there would be little enough left for them even with his insurance.

His heart, too, had leaped at the wonderful opportunity of getting treatment for Eddie, even though his pride at first forbade his accepting it. He was far more pleased than he pretended that his wife's ingenious argument would permit him to accept the doctor's offer without feeling that he was taking charity.

" I guess the boy *has* earned it," he said to himself. " He has always been a good little kid."

When, the next day, Mr. Wallace reappeared in his office, he already had made up his mind to accept even if his visitor had not brought with him a telegram from his masterful surgeon brother, which read:

" Passing through next Friday returning to New York. Have Randall boy at station. Will take him back with me.

" RALSTON WALLACE."

Friday! And to-day was Wednesday. This time it was Mrs. Randall who could hardly make up her mind to let the boy go. She had always pictured herself as sitting by Eddie's bedside when the time came for his operation. She never had thought of the possibility that Eddie might have to go through the operation alone, away from her.

"The doctor told his brother," Mr. Randall observed as they discussed Eddie's journey, "that Eddie would have to remain in the hospital from six weeks to two months. You can go on and bring him home when he is able to travel."

"But," protested Mrs. Randall, "I want to go with him. I want to be there."

"I don't see how we can afford it — that is, two trips — and if you went on and stayed there two months it would still be too expensive."

"Of course I could not do that," she admitted sadly. Anxious as her mother heart was for her youngest she realized that there was little need for her to accompany Eddie. Dr. Wallace would see that he arrived safely. Besides she would be needed at home to look after the other two boys — and their father, too. It would be much better to make the trip later to bring Eddie home.

"You don't suppose," she asked tearfully, "that there is any danger of Eddie's not surviving the operation, do you?"

"Oh, pooh, don't be silly," her husband answered. "It's a tedious treatment rather than a dangerous one. The operation is quite simple."

"But the ether — I'm afraid of his heart."

"There's nothing the matter with his heart," her husband answered. "His heart's as strong as anybody's. All that is the matter with him is his lame leg."

So four days later Eddie, all by himself, lay in a little white cot in a pleasant room in a great new hospital building. The operation was over. His leg, now all swathed in a cast of plaster, had been elevated and hung suspended by cords that ran to pulleys in the ceiling, so that no movement would bring about a displacement.

Just what had happened to him he could not clearly recall. He remembered that there had been a lot of nurses in funny-looking clothes standing around. It was not in this room but in another room where he had undressed and had climbed up on a high iron table located right under a big skylight. Dr. Wallace and his assistant had come in wearing the same funny looking clothes that the nurses had on. The doctor had put on long rubber gloves. One of the nurses had taken a sponge with a paper cone over it and had held it to his nose.

He had been told to inhale and when he did there was the funniest sicky smell. There had been a succession of fleeting, wonderful dreams — what they were about he could not remember — and then he had found himself there on the cot all strapped up, feeling very weak and sick.

"Will I be lame now?" was the first question he had asked his nurse.

It was a terrible disappointment to him when Miss Fay — she was his own particular day-nurse — explained to him that not until weeks later, until after they had taken the plaster cast off his leg, would the doctor be able to determine whether or not the operation had been successful.

Waiting day after day without knowing was hard work. Yet after the first day or two, when he had become accustomed to having his leg suspended, and had regained some of his strength, he really began to enjoy himself. So many things happened in a hospital and it was all so different from things at home. Besides, every one was so nice to him.

In the morning when he awoke there was always the incident of the night-nurse going off duty and Miss Fay coming on. The night nurse was nice but he liked Miss Fay better and always welcomed her reappearance. After his face had been washed breakfast was brought to him on a little white tray. At first Miss Fay had to feed him but he soon learned how to eat lying down. Each morning, too, there was always Dr. Wallace's visit to look forward to. Before he would realize it it was luncheon time. In the afternoon the ward surgeon, Dr. Henderson, always dropped in. Every day there came a letter from Mother and also an occasional one from Dad or one of his brothers. Once in a while a bouquet of flowers arrived bearing a card, " With Diana Wallace's compliments." He wondered and wondered how she could send the flowers all the way from home and still have them so fresh and fragrant on their arrival, never suspecting that it was really Diana's doctor uncle who was doing it. The doctor was a great believer in keeping his patients cheerful and had discovered the value of bouquets for that purpose.

By and by as he grew stronger he made the acquaintance of some of the other nurses on the floor, Miss Wilson, Miss Edgar, and Miss Jones. He liked them all and all of them made quite a fuss over him.   When they were not too busy or were off duty they got into the habit of dropping in to read to him or to play checkers with him.   From them he heard about his neighbors — about the little girl in Room 26 who had been born with club-feet, and how Dr. Wallace had straightened them out so that now she could walk as well as any one else.   There was a little boy there, too, who had been run over by an automobile and had lost both his feet.   There were other children with great humps on their backs — scores of other little patients, all of them, it seemed to Eddie, far worse off than he ever had been. When he heard about some of the others it made him feel much ashamed that he had ever resented being called "Limpy."   He never before had realized how much worse conditions there were than being a little bit lame in one leg.

"And lots of the children," said Miss Fay as he confided his feelings to her, "are orphans.   They have neither father nor mother to look out for them."

"I guess that's the worst of all," said Eddie thoughtfully.   "I am glad I have mine."

One day there came a surprise package.   It

was all done up in brown paper and tied with coarse twine. The address was written in a cramped, shaky hand. Eddie turned it over and over, wondering what it contained and who could have sent it. At last he had Miss Fay open it for him. There, inside a cigar-box, was a wonderful wooden chain of eight links, all carved out of one piece of wood.

The minute Eddie laid eyes on it he recognized the work at once.

" Why, it's from Mr. Jonas! " he exclaimed delightedly.

" Who's Mr. Jonas? " asked Miss Fay curiously.

He told her all about the old one-legged man and what wonderful chums they were and how once, when the family moved, he had stayed for a whole week with Jonas.

The third week he found that by twisting himself around a little in the bed he could write on a pad with a lead pencil. After that he conducted a voluminous correspondence. He wrote to his Mother, to Dad, to his brothers, to little Diana Wallace to thank her for the flowers, and several times he wrote to old Jonas, telling him all about life in the hospital.

One morning he heard Dr. Wallace say to Miss Fay:

"To-morrow I'm going to take off the plaster."

After the doctor had gone out of the room he lay silent and still for a long time, a question trembling on his lips that he hardly dared to ask.

"Will he know then?" he asked at length.

"Know what, Eddie dear?" said Miss Fay.

He gulped once or twice before he could put the question into words. It was such an all-important question.

"Whether I'm going to be lame any more."

"We hope so," the nurse replied. "We all hope so."

All that afternoon and evening he had little to say and the nurses that night among themselves had quite a discussion as to how he would take the news if the doctor told him that his lame leg was to be all right.

"Of course," said Miss Fay cautiously, "there is always the possibility of the operation being a failure. The muscles may not read-just themselves to the new conditions properly. I think Eddie's heart will be just broken if everything is not all right. He looks at me so wistfully that I know he keeps wondering and worrying about it although he never asks any questions."

" The doctor has performed that operation so often," said Miss Jones, " that I don't think there is much likelihood of his having failed this time. How do you suppose Eddie will take it when he learns that he is not to be lame? "

" I know the first thing he will want to do," said Miss Fay. " He will want to write a letter."

" I expect you are right," said Miss Jones. " He will want to write to his mother at once and tell her that he is cured."

" His first letter will not be to his mother," argued Miss Edgar. " He has such appreciation and gratitude for everything that is done for him that I'm sure his very first act will be to write a letter of thanks to the doctor's niece. She's really responsible for his being here."

" You can't tell about boys," insisted Miss Wilson. " They say the bond between father and son is always strong. I wouldn't be surprised if he wrote his father first."

" All of you are wrong," insisted Miss Fay. " He'll write first to that old Mr. Jonas, I believe he thinks more of him than he does of his own family. He's that old one-legged man who sent him the wooden chain. They are wonderful pals. He tells that old man things he wouldn't tell his own mother and father."

The morning came. The plaster cast was removed. For many minutes Dr. Wallace's deft fingers felt and massaged and explored the muscles of the youngster's limb. Eddie silently watched him, his eyes glistening with suppressed excitement as he waited for the verdict. Miss Fay fluttered about the room, almost as much wrought up as was her patient. Outside the door in the corridor, gathered close that they might quickly hear the news, was the little group of nurses who had become Eddie's particular friends.

At last the surgeon spoke.

" Well, young man," he said, and Miss Fay's experienced eye read in his expression that he was well satisfied with the result of his operation, " you're through with that brace forever. In a few months you'll be walking as well as any one, with hardly a limp."

Eddie tried to thank the doctor but something choked in his throat and he could not

speak. Even after the doctor had left the
room he just lay there smiling happily.

"Are you glad, Eddie?" asked Miss Fay.

He could not trust himself yet to speak even
to her. It seemed as if years and years he had
been carrying a great big bundle on his shoulders that kept him tired all the time and some
one had suddenly lifted it off. He lay there
silent, happily contemplating the possibilities
of life with two legs instead of a leg and a half.
How grand it would be never again to be called
"Limpy!" Nobody would ever bother him
again asking him what made him lame. He
could play ball now and climb trees and do all
the other things his brothers were accustomed
to do.

With tears, unrestrainable tears of joy,
welling up in his eyes, he turned to his
nurse.

"Please, Miss Fay," he asked, "may I
write a letter?"

Smiling triumphantly that her prediction as
to his first act had thus far come true she gave
him a pad and pencil. For a few minutes he
wrote steadily with forehead wrinkled and lips
puckered. As he finished his note a new light
shone in his eyes.

"Will you please mail that for me right away?" he asked, handing it to her to be put in an envelope and addressed, as she did with all his letters.

As she went out of the room to get an envelope the other nurses crowded around her, eager to see the letter.

"Who's it to?" they asked.

"His mother?"

"His father?"

"Little Diana Wallace?"

"Old Mr. Jonas?"

Miss Fay shook her head to all of them and silently extended the note for them to read.

After all, what does womankind know of the inner workings of a boy's mind? How can women understand or appreciate a boy's secret thoughts? What part have women in a boy's dearest ambitions? Even a boy's own mother, who sees him every day, cannot always understand him.

Eddie's letter, his first letter when he found that he was no longer to wear a brace, was never again to be "Limpy" Randall, was addressed to a former adversary in the town where he used to live. It read:

" *Dear Froggie Sweeney:*

"I, Edward Haverford Randall, challenge you. I'm not lame any more. As soon as I get out of the hospital I'll fight you any day and place you name."

"The very idea," exclaimed Miss Jones. "Wanting to fight the very first thing! Aren't boys terrible?"

But old Jonas could have told her that for years Eddie had been a valiant fighter. Just having to live is a fight for the lame.

THE END

Printed in the United States
25053LVS00001B/53